Manchester Lake

A Darkly Enchanted Romance

Joshua Ian

MOODY BOXFAN
BOOKS

Moody Boxfan Books

Contents

EPIGRAPH

"**A** water nymph does not get much novelty."

The Mermaid of Druid Lake (1906)
By Charles Weathers Bump

PREFACE

"On a night my love strode the banks"
Author Unknown

On a night my love strode the banks, by the waters
opal black
And talked to me of our hearts that might not ever
be the same
Time was lost, duty forgot, home was a place I
never wanted back
We thought to run away and flee, until the dawn,
at last, she came

And with her rosy fingers wove the clouds
Into a morn just like a shroud
Worn most to cover up our shame
With hope that none would know our names

Escape by boat all day we planned, so we kept the
waters near
But the waves and ripples mocked us like a mirror
glass that shon

It sought to show the world truth; it cast reflections of us clear

Our future sealed and not for dreams, we longed again for the dawn

And how her rosy fingers wove the clouds
Into a morn just like a shroud
Which we pulled close in contented shame
And cursed the world for its need of names

Oh, I recall

That night my love strode down the banks by waters opal black

And told me of our hearts and how we might ne'er get them back

Chapter One

EPILOGUE: Paris, 1907

Monty had lost track of time and was unsure how long he had been wandering the city. He had finally come to rest on one of the footpaths of the *Pont Alexandre III*. It was not so late in the evening that he was alone, he could see a small crowd of people milling near the *Grand Palais* at the other end of the bridge. Two carriages made their way behind him in crossing, and at the nearest intersection he watched as a steam bus carrying only a handful of passengers rattled by. He leaned against the railing of the bridge and gazed out over the near-invisible Seine. It caught the lights of the city and sparkled in places as its waves lapped lazily, but most of the river looked an immense cloak of black, swallowed up by the night, only the dim moon reflected back.

The soft motion of the midnight water soothed him. The faint sound of it like a low song to calm his spirit. How welcome the river just below him seemed, like a thick, warm blanket on a cold evening. He might just wrap himself up in it and escape, sleep forever and be far away from the pain of his heartbreak.

When the tears came, he at first did not feel or notice them. They fell like small crystals catching the glint of moonlight, and then consumed by darkness. A sob tore across his chest but he held it back, determined not to let any passersby hear evidence of his despair. Instead, he wept silently, his torso shaking slightly against the stone parapet of the bridge. To steady himself he began to hum the tune he had heard in the café just a few days before.

Those few days seemed now like a lifetime ago. His small song echoed back to him from below, the sound reverberating through the arched supports of the underside of the bridge, tumbling down to the surface and back up. He stopped his vocalizations, and just listened. The echo stopped and then a moment later he heard his song repeated, only now it seemed deeper in tone, more throaty and ethereal. The cadence lasted but a few seconds and stopped, and even in his distraught state, he thought it queer how the water had thrown the sound back upon him.

Lifting his head, he gazed up at one of the gilded winged horses at the end of the bridge. What a thing it must be, to be a creature of myth. To outlast human concern and necessity and to be able to ascend, at any moment, and take to the skies. Fleeing attachment, fleeing time, and just to be unfettered; to be utterly free.

He stood, wiping his face. Inhaling deeply, he nodded and straightened his clothing.

"Right," he declared softly. "Enough of that."

He looked out over the river once again and shook his head against its appeal. He would be leaving Paris soon and, with it, the site of his heartbreak. If he decided to, he knew that he might never have to revisit either Paris or his heartbreak again, no matter how beautifully either appealed. There were so many wondrous places to visit in the world, he assured himself, and so many chances at love. But he wished he could believe that just now. Just now he wanted never to see another handsome face, never to hear another lovely song, never to gaze upon another thing of beauty. It was all too much.

He turned and began his walk down the footpath. He considered stopping by one of the many bars he would pass, but decided against it. Back to the hotel, only that, to sleep. Sleep, sleep, sleep.

Just as he reached the corner, he thought he heard a noise behind him, coming from out over the water. A noise that sounded somehow like his name, his name being called like a song. He turned around and peered out over the Seine. There was nothing he could see below but the water. The noise drifted to him again, a low note, like a humming, that wrapped itself into his name. Monty, it seemed to say. He looked around but saw no one. Across the river and some ways further down, a lantern was lit on a parked boat. He saw two men roaming about on the deck of the barge in the shadows of the light. That must be it, he told himself, that he had only overheard their chatter, morphed by the distance. He turned again to leave and as he took a step, he heard a large splashing sound directly behind and he paused.

Every little thing seemed to be getting to him, he decided. His nerves were raw, his emotions exhausted. He must sleep, rest his mind.

And so he left the sounds of the river behind him and moved on.

Chapter Two

Dubaney House, Essex, England, 1910

"It's a Baker Electric," declared Bishop proudly, smacking his hand on the padded bench seat. "A Victoria model."

"It's rather a unique shape, isn't it?" replied Monty.

"Yes, it is," Bishop beamed. "I paid extra to have her kitted out just so. I don't think there's another like it anywhere."

Monty examined the vehicle. He watched his old friend Bishop strut around it like a proud parent might an exemplary child. Occasionally he took a rag from his back pocket and polished a bit of black metal or the overhead bonnet. It was a marvelous contraption, no matter how much he did not let on to Bishop that he thought. This particular model reminded him of the electric wagons, mainly used for postal service or other sorts of deliveries that he often saw in the streets of London only in truncated form.

"And what does it do exactly?" he asked.

"It's an automobile, Monty. It doesn't do anything, it simply goes."

Monty thought back to all the many catalogs Bishop had shown him, as he extolled the virtues of this vehicle or that one, and knew this one might have cost as much as ten times that of a good horse.

"Yes, I do realize that, dear Bishop. But what I mean is, although it is grand, it's rather small. Does it somehow *go* differently from other vehicles? For the price couldn't you have gotten something bigger or at least more practical?"

"Rubbish to 'practical'. I expect you must have seen quite a few of these during your months in America?"

"Yes, actually I did," said Monty. "Mostly in New York I tried to walk, to take in all the sights, and I liked the underground railway. It was like getting lost in an entirely new world. But there were many of these automobiles about. On occasion I even took one of those cabs, with the French name?"

"The Darracq cabs? Fabulous little machine, I'm told."

"Yes, they were quite charming. Bright red and the drivers all dressed up like royal cadets or butlers or some such."

"Much better than those American smoke-wagons. I have it on good word that electric vehicles are the future. Those fuel-based engines won't stick around. Trust me, you'll see."

"Will I?"

"Besides," Bishop continued. "I like that I don't need a driver. I can take her out all by myself. It gives one a sense of freedom to be able to just take off and go whenever I please, and to not always have someone—a chauffeur or some other agent of my parents—attending and keeping track of my comings and goings."

"As to your comings and goings, I should think the most renowned accounting agency would have trouble keeping track."

"I'll take that as the compliment I am sure it was meant," said Bishop with a wink. "Now change into your driving clothes, I've had Cook prepare us a picnic lunch. There's something I want to show you at Manchester Lake."

"Bishop, you know very well I do not possess *driving* clothes." Monty possessed two tweed day suits appropriate for the country and one linen, but it was far too cool for that at the moment. "And although I do love the lake, isn't it a bit early in the season for bathing?"

"We shan't be bathing. Unless, that is, you enjoy bathing with wild animals?"

Monty's curiosity was piqued but he wouldn't let on.

"Well, I have been bathing with you on frequent occasions, so obviously I do not object to wild animals," Monty retorted with a devious smile.

"Why, you terrible bitch," said Bishop with a laugh. "Come, my dear silver-tongued brother, egg cress and lemonade await us."

"There is no end to your generosity, I see."

Monty eyed the little buggy, with its great bulging head lamps and snub-nosed front end staring back at him like some silly voiceless storybook creature, and hoped it was safer than most of Bishop's faddish obsessions.

Bishop, of course, did change into driving clothes after wresting the car from its charging station that had been constructed in the back courtyard of Dubaney House. In his tweed Norfolk suit and cap, he looked the picture of a country racing car driver to Monty. Racing car driver only in that he insisted on ripping through the estate at top speed, despite the narrowness of a passage or type of earth on which they were hurled.

Monty clutched at his own straw boater, which threatened to take off from his head, and squeezed his calves tightly on either side of the picnic basket resting between them as Bishop turned one particularly precarious curve with glee.

"Mamma's still quite scared of electricity, you know," explained Bishop in a raised voice. "She hated when Father turned the house over to electric. She's frightened to death one of the bulbs is going to explode when she enters a room. She still carries a lamp in the evenings. But luckily Father persisted, so I was able to have this beauty."

As Monty took stock of Bishop's driving skills, he couldn't say that he blamed Bishop's mother for any wariness. But, despite the fact that he worried the put upon little metal beast might at any moment explode, Monty had to admit it was exhilarating to drive thusly.

"This thing you plan to show me at the lake? It is a timed event? You seem to be in an awful hurry."

"Not at all," said Bishop. "But it does rather come and goes as it pleases, so I'm not entirely sure when it will show up next."

"'It'? What exactly is it?"

"A seal."

Monty was thrown. "I beg your pardon?"

"At least I think it's a seal," added Bishop. "Or perhaps it is a walrus? I don't really know the difference."

"Have you gone barmy on the crumpet?" asked Monty.

"How dare you. I am as sane as they come. For the most part." Bishop shrugged. "No, there is a seal in Manchester Lake, I swear to you. Or possibly a sea lion of some sort. It is rather large. I'm not particularly an expert on these things."

"I shouldn't expect you to be. But how in Heaven's name did a seal—or a walrus or whatever it may be—get into Manchester Lake?"

"Damned if I know," Bishop said with a shake of the head. "I assume he swam there. You know there is an outlet to the Thames estuary on one side of it."

"But why? How?"

"Well, they like the cold, don't they? And it does promise to be a very cold winter."

"I'm not entirely sure that it works that way, dear Bishop."

"Perhaps it's a porpoise then. Seals and porpoises are quite the same aren't they?"

"I believe not at all," Monty clucked his tongue. "Obviously it is just the Loch Ness monster come for a visit."

"All the way from Scotland? That's awfully far to swim I should think."

"As opposed to Antarctica?" asked Monty with a roll of his eyes.

"Blimey, is that where they find seals? That's even further than Scotland, isn't it?"

"Yes, Bishop. Only just."

After some rather unremarkable sandwiches and a gorgeous apple tart afterwards, they settled onto the grass and talked, all the while sipping champagne, which had been kept cool in the currents of the water. They spent the better part of two languid hours by the lake. The weather was perfect that day, the air dry and crisp, the sun warming despite the cooling temperatures of the season.

After refilling his glass, Monty laid himself down beside Bishop who was leaned on his elbows staring out at the water. Even the small bit of sun they'd had flushed his pale cheeks, and his ginger hair, cut close with longish sideburns, glinted in its light.

"Still no sign of your seal," Monty said.

"No," said Bishop, with a sharp shake of his head. "And it's dashed annoying. I had hoped to show you; it seemed like something you would enjoy."

"Am I known to be fond of seals?"

"Don't be silly, Monty, of course not. But we've spent more time by this lake during your visits than anywhere else on the estate. You know what you're like about water. I first saw the creature a couple of months ago and then it disappeared. I thought possibly I had created it in my mind. But then just last week when I received word of your return, I drove by the lake, hoping for a sighting. And, sure as you know it, there was the creature, jumping out of the water and practically twirling."

"Maybe it is a porpoise then?"

"Whatever it is, it's jolly to see." Bishop sighed. "Testament, I imagine, to the fact that there has been far too little resembling entertainment out here."

"Yes, that is a thing, isn't it?"

"What's that?"

"How you've managed to survive almost six months in the country with your parents. In all the years I've known you, you've hardly spent that much time here, even during summer breaks. You never did explain why you up and left London so suddenly."

"Oh, Monty, you're being dramatic. It was not sudden."

"I beg your pardon, but I distinctly remember going to your apartments—which I remind you, you had been renting for the better part of a year—and your landlord informed me that you had packed up everything and gone to the country. It had only been four days since I'd seen you last, and you typically tell me everything."

"I sometimes wonder if I don't tell you too much."

"It was sudden and bizarre, and, to be honest, I was a little hurt."

"I apologize, Monty, I really do. What can I say? I had suddenly simply had too much of the city. I felt the need to get out, to escape."

"To run away, more like. Whose heart had you crushed and left to hunt you down for revenge?"

Bishop gave him a quick look. "Nothing like that. I simply felt the need for space and air. I am capricious, what can I say? I always have been, you know this of me. I'm sure it's one of the qualities about me that make me ever so interesting, in fact."

Monty rolled his eyes in exasperation, and flopped onto his back.

"The other quality I find endlessly fascinating about you is your ability to completely and utterly delude yourself as to your faults. That is an endless feast of enjoyment."

"You bitch," Bishop said with affected hurt. Then he grinned and elbowed Monty sharply in the side.

"Are you sure your parents won't mind me staying here for a bit?" asked Monty.

"Not at all. They adore you. All those summers you spent here during school, they grew quite fond of you. Not to mention, you provide much more interesting dinner conversation than I."

Monty smiled. "Only because I listen to them."

"And that is only because you didn't spend your life with them. But what of your parents, come to that? Won't they miss you in London? You've only just got back from America."

"Possibly. But then they do like being able to say their son is staying at Dubaney House. Very on the up on all those social connections."

"Oh, pish. Isn't your father connected to the Raj or something?"

Monty gave a chuckle. "Only via a distant cousin, somehow. Most of his family are just humble businessmen like him."

"The great Mister Rajit Singer?" Bishop chuckled now. "Your father is many things but humble is not one of them."

"No, I suppose not."

Monty leaned backed onto his elbows and looked out over the landscape contemplatively.

"Do you miss America terribly?" asked Bishop after a moment.

"I suppose I do." Monty nodded. "It was only four months, I know, but it was like stepping into an entirely new version of myself. Which I think I had been craving for quite some time." He reached over and grabbed a small notebook from the pocket of his jacket. "And I got a lot of lovely drawings out of it."

He waved the sketchbook in the air.

"I imagine you just did," said Bishop, grabbing for it. "I suppose you won't show me any of your drawings, as usual."

"Correct."

"Who knows what manner of half-dressed docks man or train porter you managed to add to your pages under the guise of character study." Bishop glanced at him slyly. "Did you seduce one of those sparkling red cabbie drivers?"

Monty sniffed. "You know, Bishop, not everyone sees every new environment as a landscape for sexual conquest."

"Rubbish."

"And I was there for my classes. To study art."

Bishop rolled his eyes and settled back onto the grass, putting his arms behind his head.

"You're not as innocent as all that, Montgomery Singer. And I'll have you know I've been living practically like a monk during my recent time in the country."

"You mean your mother has invited no young men of interest to her many dinner parties."

"I said *practically* like a monk, not *entirely*."

"Touché."

Bishop drifted off into an afternoon nap and Monty opened his sketchbook. He took in the scene before him and began to sketch it. It was always a meditative act, drawing, and he often lost himself in the mere physicality of sketching. Today was such a day, and when he looked down at the page, he was surprised by what he saw. It was the scene before him, the lake and the sloping hills that came to meet it. But sat just on the edge of the lake, he had drawn the form of a man. And when he studied it, he realized it was his mystery man.

He shook his head in wonder. It had been happening again of late. He was back again, the mysterious faceless man at the end of his pencil. For years this figure had haunted the corners of his mind but he had never been able to draw him out completely formed. Often he got the body quite correct, the shapeliness of his musculature, the lines of his shoulders and hips. Occasionally the full lips, the strong nose. But never did it all come together as a whole.

Yet he was still compelled at times to draw this figure, almost as if he had no control over the desire. Like automatic writing or something otherwise akin to it, his hand would move over the paper, fashioning the form of this unknown man. He wrote it off to his spending too much time in art galleries studying technique, and, quite possibly, the limits of his own talents.

The man had disappeared from his pages for quite some time. Three years, in fact. And had only started reappearing again on his return to England from America. Until then he had not made an appearance since France, and that trip that to this day still caused Bishop to button up as tight as a corset whenever it was mentioned.

But why again now?

"What are you drawing?" asked Bishop, sleepily, interrupting his ruminating.

"Oh, nothing, just the lake and the trees."

"Not the most fascinating subject, I imagine."

"No, not the most." Monty closed the book and wound the closing ribbon around it. "Bishop, I have been meaning to ask. Have you had any strange memories of late? Things you thought you had forgotten springing back up?"

Bishop seemed to tense. He sat and gave Monty an odd look.

"What do you mean?" he asked tightly.

"Only I've been thinking about things lately. Things I thought I had left behind me. Things from our time in France, particularly."

Bishop turned away from him.

"You know I don't like to talk about France, Monty. And I should think you would want to put it well behind you."

"Yes, I know. But I can't help thinking of it, and it seems to haunt me lately—"

There was a loud sound then, like the bark of an animal but which reverberated like the smack of cymbals, and then a splash.

"What was that?" Monty asked.

"What?" Bishop echoed, turning his attention back to Monty.

Another splash, louder than the other, was followed by two cracks of sounds, new barks.

They both peered out at the lake.

A wide grin broke across Bishop's face.

"Why, it's that damned seal. Finally!"

They were both up in a flash and hurrying down to the banks of the lake. Bishop was pointing, laughing.

"There it is!" he cried, laughing. "Monty, I told you."

Dumbfounded, Monty shook his head.

"Good lord," he exclaimed. "It's enormous."

It did, in fact, appear to be a seal, and, in fact, an enormous one. Not to mention energetic. The length of the thing appeared to be at least the height of an average man, and it was doing some movement similar to a hop that had it flinging itself to and fro in the water, with great splashes, much to Bishop's enjoyment. Monty moved closer to the lake to examine it.

The lovely brown creature seemed to be satisfied that it was being paid attention to and ceased with its bounding. It moved into something like a backstroke and then dipped under the surface. When it reappeared, it was but a few feet away and it swam towards Monty, where it paused just at the bank's edge. It looked up at Monty, who smiled, and then it inhaled sharply. Staring back at Monty were two large brown eyes. But these were not the ordinary eyes of a horse or even an intelligent dog; these eyes seemed entirely too human to be believed. They did not shine with animal joy, but rather regarded him deeply. *Regarded*, that was the only word he could come up with to describe it to himself. It seemed that the creature was appraising him with quite a critical eye. But Monty felt no discomfort at this, instead, for some reason, he felt a great connection with the creature, some sort of recognition that was returned to him.

"Why, he's marvelous," said Monty.

The seal creature issued a large, loud bark then, filled with what seemed to be joy, and Monty could have sworn he saw the thing smile.

"Didn't I tell you?" said Bishop proudly. "A real live seal. In our very own Manchester Lake."

Monty watched the creature swim around in a tight circle and wondered at Bishop's appraisal. It did resemble a seal, as well as he knew, but there was something about it that suggested it was something else entirely. Its size, for one thing, but also the way its body stretched out and the texture of its skin, which seemed not at all as coarse as he imagined it ought to be. It also had no whiskers on its face, a trait he thought common in most cold-weather aquatic creatures, and then again, of course, were those eyes.

Those eyes that were again studying him. It was as if the creature were waiting on him to make a decision. Monty smiled at the creature and nodded to let it know that everything was fine, that they meant no harm.

"Should we feed it something, do you think?" asked Bishop. "We've some leftover tart, I believe. Or maybe some egg sandwich?"

"I'm not sure that is what seals typically eat," Monty said. "I would assume seals eat fish or seaweed or some such as that. I doubt very much— Bishop? Why are you making that face?"

Bishop began to laugh and Monty turned to follow his friend's gaze.

"It looks like he wants more than lunch," said Bishop.

The creature had somehow managed to propel itself onto the green grass surrounding the lake and was moving past them. He—and for some reason Monty felt sure it was a he—paused in his trek across the field when he seemed to notice their stares. Looking back at them, he issued a short bright bark and once again began his trudge over the grass.

"Where in the world is he going?" Monty asked.

"I'll be damned, but I think he's heading towards the Baker," said Bishop who had already started after the creature.

Monty shook his head in confusion but followed his friend, who had at this point broken into a light jog as the seal seemed to be advancing at an extraordinary pace.

"For having no legs, the bloody thing can move," cried Bishop.

What could he want with the automobile? How could he even have seen it from the lake, come to that? But nevertheless he seemed to be making a straight line for it. The two friends ran slightly ahead of the creature and stood by the car to see if he bypassed it, but indeed he stopped just at it.

Sat there by its curved foot runner, the seal seemed to rear back. It was as if he were trying to catapult his long tubular body into the horseless carriage. Unable to overcome the high frame of the vehicle, he fell back to the ground and gave them an imploring glance. He barked at them, twisting his head in a motion that seemed as if he were indicating the car.

"I think the chappie wants a ride," said Bishop, on the verge of laughter. "I'll say this much, the beggar's got good taste in the end."

Monty was acutely more hesitant. Something about the level of intelligence this creature displayed seemed a bit disarming. He hung back as his friend stepped towards the vehicle.

"Well, come on," said Bishop. "Help me get him up."

"What? Where?"

"Into the Baker, of course."

"Do you think that's wise?" asked Monty, still hesitant.

"What could it harm? If he settles to it, I'll give him a short ride around the estate."

The seal barked then, and reared back, bobbing his head.

"You see, he wants to go for a drive," declared Bishop.

The creature issued another bright bark, and when Monty glanced over, it seemed to be staring just at him again. Its eyes were bright, and, dare he think it, almost mischievous-looking.

"I suppose it couldn't hurt," conceded Monty, with a chuckle.

He helped Bishop pick the massive creature up and, as carefully as they could, they set him down on the floor of the vehicle. Its tail, the back flippers, Monty supposed they were called, hung out of the side of the car. As Monty was releasing his arms from the weight and standing, he swore he felt a small, wet kiss on his face, as if the creature had licked him.

He it was surprised to be sure, but the seal had settled himself on the floorboard and appeared to have a somewhat worried expression on its face. Just then it began to shiver wildly, quivering with ripples of motion. The poor thing looked suddenly stricken and hunched into itself.

"Good lord," Monty said. "I think the thing's gone ill. Ought we to return him to the lake?"

But as Bishop and Monty leaned in towards it, the great seal let out another bark, different in tone, and slunk back against the baseboard, trying to evade their reach.

"He doesn't seem to want to go," said Bishop.

"But look at him," said Monty. "He's wracked with shivers."

"Perhaps..." said Bishop, thinking. "Aha!"

He jogged around to the back of the Baker and retrieved a driving blanket that had been tucked behind the bench seat.

"Let's wrap him in this," he suggested. "And maybe it will help."

Monty shrugged, thinking of no better solution, and they tried to swaddle the oddly shaped creature as best they could with the blanket. The creature seemed doleful but somewhat more comfortable, even though it still shook like an autumn tree in a storm. It looked up at them with a doe-eyed expression and issued a soft, nudging bark.

"Come on," said Bishop. "Let's clean up our lunch. Once we're packed, we can see if the thing still wants a ride and, if not, we'll carry him back to the lake."

Monty nodded, although reluctant to leave the creature, and trotted back to their picnic spot.

As they returned to the Baker, basket and blanket in hand, Monty felt a slight niggle of worry rush over him as he noticed that the creature's tail no longer overhung the side of the vehicle. He called out, making a noise somewhat like a bark, hoping the creature would answer in turn.

"What are you about?" asked a bemused Bishop.

Monty shrugged. Not sure why he had felt the need to try to communicate with their creature in its own language.

"I am worried our new friend has fled the scene," he said.

"Really?" Bishop examined the vehicle more closely. "Maybe so. Perhaps he's just somehow climbed up onto the riding bench."

As they got closer to the car, both young men went slack-jawed. Instead of the massive seal they had wrestled into the car, there, on the seat, sat a very tall and broad-shouldered man wrapped in the very same driving blanket Bishop had retrieved.

Bishop was slack-jawed, but Monty backed away from the car, frowning.

He couldn't believe his eyes. There, sat on the bench, was the man from his sketchbook. At least, that is, the man he saw in his mind as he struggled to put the image on paper. The very same features which had sometimes crowded his dreams were just there. Real and in the flesh.

And indeed he was exactly how Monty had imagined. Quite the most beautiful man he had ever seen. Deeply bronzed skin, dark curly hair, and shimmering brown eyes with flecks of gold. Eyes he recognized. They were the same eyes that had studied him in the lake, but now they looked even more familiar. As if he had gazed on them many a time over in his dreams.

On the one hand, Monty wanted to touch him, to feel him, to trace the lines he had so often dashed off in pencil that were now made manifest. But, on the other hand, fear won out. How in the world could this be? What sort of sorcery was it that some man he had only imagined was before him? Obviously strange things happened—like giant seals throwing themselves from the water and crawling to automobiles. But how could this be?

"Selkie!" Monty blurted out.

The man in the car bowed his head bashfully and smiled.

Bishop seemed to have been shaken loose from his shock.

"What are you saying?" he asked.

"A s-s-selkie," repeated Monty. "He must be a selkie."

The man motioned for them to come closer, though he did not rise from the seat. Bishop, his mouth still agape, walked towards the car.

"Bishop," Monty cautioned. "Be careful."

Chapter Three

"What the bloody hell is a selkie?" cried Bishop, one eye on the man in the car.

"A mythical creature, Scottish I believe, or possibly Norse, from the sea," Monty explained. "They look like seals but when they come ashore, they take human form. The females are said to be extraordinary wives, and the males are said to excel in—" He glanced over at the man in the car who seemed to be listening very intently.

"Well, in the art of seduction," Monty concluded in a whisper. He ignored what he swore was a smile curling the lips of the man-creature before him.

"Are they dangerous?" asked Bishop.

"Not to my knowledge. But, of course, how could I know? I didn't think they actually existed. All we have are stories, and the stories don't say anything about them doing anyone harm."

"Well, you certainly seemed to have been hesitant when you saw him."

"A strange man—a strange, naked man, at that—suddenly appeared in the backseat of your automobile? It is slightly disconcerting, don't you think?"

"So you believe us to have found a mythical creature swimming in an English country lake? It seems an awful leap."

"I suppose so. But given all the evidence, I can't explain it any other way. Besides, there is something about his eyes…"

"His eyes? Good lord, Monty. Do you mean to tell me you can deduce sorcery from a comely glance?"

"Of course not, Bishop. But what other explanation can there be? There is no seal about and I think we certainly might have noticed a man such as this running up out of nowhere. In the end, is it really any less believable than a seal or a porpoise swanning around your lake?"

"In that seals and porpoises actually exist," answered Bishop, "Yes, I think it is rather."

Monty dipped his head in concession. "I take your point."

They peered at the man in the car who studied them both with open and intelligent curiosity.

"And you," Bishop said, pointing at the man. "What do you have to say to all this?"

The man looked at him with wide eyes and then gave a little shake of his head. He then patted the seat beside him, clearing inviting Bishop to have a seat. Bishop began to approach the vehicle.

"Bishop," Monty warned. "What are you doing?"

"He looks harmless enough."

"He looks as if he could snap your neck easily," said Monty.

Bishop shrugged. "I've experience with those types."

Bishop came up to the side of the car, and the man inside reached out a hand and laid it softly on Bishop's shoulder before withdrawing it again.

"There, you see," said Bishop. "Rather gentle, in fact."

Monty's instincts told him that the man did, in fact, seem gentle. But there was something about him that frightened Monty still. The coincidence was too odd a thing.

"What do you suppose we should do with him then?" asked Monty.

Bishop shrugged, sighing. "Take him for that drive, I suppose."

The man in the car smiled and nodded.

"That doesn't seem wise at all," Monty protested.

The selkie gave him a look but Monty turned quickly away. The man's mournful eyes had actually moved him and he was annoyed with himself to have been so moved.

"We can't very well toss a full-grown male into a lake," said Bishop.

"But he isn't a man; he's a selkie. Selkies can swim. As we have only just seen all too well."

"My god, Monty. No matter what he is, we can't just leave the man out here, naked and mute. What has come over you?"

Monty came closer to the automobile and spoke in hushed tones.

"So you object to the existence of mythical creatures, but not to giving them rides in your new automobile?"

"What harm can it do?" Bishop gave a cheeky smile. "We can see he has no concealed weapons on his person."

Timidly glancing down the fine form only covered to about the elbows by the driving blanket, Monty wasn't so sure he entirely agreed with that assessment.

He slapped Bishop on the shoulder. "Concentrate, Bishop. I am uncertain. This feels very queer."

Bishop crossed his arms.

"He seems very keen to ride in my car—and who could blame him, it is a beauty. If he tries anything funny, we'll bring him back here and have nothing more to do with him. He's quite the figure, but I imagine the both of us might be able to handle him and a driving blanket. Show a sense of adventure, Monty. If he is indeed a sealky as you say—"

"Selkie."

"Yes, yes, whatever. If he is one, then are you really going to turn down the opportunity to know him? Who knows, maybe he has appeared to show you a wonder of things you've never known."

Monty chewed on his bottom lip and studied the magnificent creature in the car.

"That's precisely what I'm worried about," he muttered.

"Come on then, old man."

"You know, you seem awfully well-adjusted to the fact that there is a mythical creature sitting in your automobile, Bishop."

Bishop shrugged. "I've seen stranger things."

"Have you indeed? Stranger things than a magically transforming man?"

Bishop looked at him for a moment, and the look was not one of amusement. It seemed as if he wanted to say something very serious to Monty. Then a flash of emotion crossed his face and he returned to his usual cheerful self.

"Oh, do shut up and get in the car, Monty."

Monty did climb in, seating himself on the other side of the selkie so that he was sandwiched between him and Bishop. He reached up and removed the blanket from the selkie's shoulders and spread it across his lap.

"That's better then," said Monty. "And do keep your hands in your lap where we can see them, please. Do you understand?"

The selkie rested his hands in his lap and gave Monty a coy smile.

"Goodness," Monty whispered, caught by the beauty of the fellow.

Maybe, he thought to himself, he had overreacted just a tad. After all, the resemblance must surely be a coincidence, mustn't it? How could the man of his dreams have been swimming in Manchester Lake all this time?

Monty shook his head and looked away. How, indeed. Monty chided himself back to good sense. And how could it be that the creature sitting here might even be the *man* of his dreams when not too long ago he was a great beast splashing about a lake? There couldn't be anything more ridiculous, and he felt embarrassed and ashamed to even have entertained the idea.

After a thorough drive around the estate, they presented the selkie with the option of returning to his lake home, and were met with vigorous head shaking and grunts of protest. As he seemed to understand, they tried to reassure him that they would come to visit again in future but his expression remained fierce and obstinate.

In truth, Monty found himself growing more and more curious about the creature. The initial shock of his appearance had not yet worn off, and Monty still found himself very wary, but he wanted to know more.

They sat, parked in the automobile, the manor house a distance off, deciding what to do.

"What if we take him to London?" Monty suggested.

"London?" Bishop was baffled.

"Yes." Monty wasn't entirely sure why the idea had come to him, but he was warming to it. "It would be awkward if he stayed around here, especially with your mother's dinner party tonight. We could make our excuses and head into the city."

"Mamma won't accept excuses, we'll just have to make a run for it, I suppose." Bishop looked at him.

"Can we just take him off like that? Suppose the lake is his home? Isn't that a bit like kidnapping?"

"Yes, I see your point." Monty shrugged. "But he doesn't seem particularly keen on returning to the lake at the moment. And I don't think we can keep him hidden in the house. If we set out soon in this great-grandfather-clock-on-wheels, we should be in the city in only a couple of hours, shouldn't we?"

"Yes, of course, don't be insulting," answered Bishop, slightly miffed. "The Baker is a highly powered machine and it... Blast! Do you know Monty, London is the perfect idea, after all."

"Is it?" Monty was surprised at the sudden acquiescence.

"Yes, we can take him to the Brunswick."

"The Brunswick? But why would we want to take him there, Bishop? I'm not entirely sure he is prepared for such a place as that."

"Nonsense," said Bishop. "He seems quite sturdy in all ways. And I know someone who may be able to help us. Someone who is rather studied in the manner of all things occult and weird— He can help us to decide—well, what to do with him exactly."

"What friend is this?"

"The Weaver."

"The Weaver? I wasn't aware you were friends with Daniel Weaver."

Bishop raised his brows. "'Friends' may be too strong a term, but I have made his acquaintance once or twice before. I had been meaning to seek him again. So this might be the perfect excuse."

Monty was confused by, and slightly suspicious of, this previously undisclosed friendship with the Weaver fellow. Again the idea that Bishop had been hiding something from him sprang to mind. But he knew better than to press the issue just now. Besides, an idea had begun to scratch at the back of his mind.

"Bishop, do you think this Weaver fellow might know something about premonitions?"

"I suppose he might. He seemed very much the expert in most things weird or occult."

Monty gave him a look. "I never knew you to have an interest in the occult."

"Aren't I allowed to keep any part of myself only to myself? After all, you never let me even have a peek at that bloody notebook of yours."

"Fair play."

"What say you, old chap?" Bishop turned to the selkie. "Would you like to go to London?"

The selkie nodded quite seriously.

"Do you think he understands us?" asked Bishop.

"Somehow I think he does." Monty gave him a once over. "But we certainly can't take him to London dressed in a riding blanket."

"No, of course not. We'll have to dress him first."

"How will we get into the house undetected?"

"We'll have to park at the front of the house and go in there," said Bishop.

"But won't someone see us?"

"Less of a chance there then coming in from the back courtyard."

With a nod, Bishop put the machine in gear and leapt into motion. They quickly pulled around the front drive, coming in at a reasonable speed so as not to make much noise on the crushed shell.

For modesty's sake, Monty and Bishop tried arranging the driving blanket, along with the picnic blanket they had stowed, into the form of some ersatz toga as best they could before rushing through the front door. They were just crossing the foyer when they heard a voice. It was Mister Beaufort, the butler.

"Oh, hello, sir, I didn't realize you— Oh, sir!"

Beaufort came to a sudden halt and stared at the trio.

"Hello, Beaufort," said Bishop in his best conciliatory tones. "Don't mind us. Things will be things sometimes, you know how us chaps operate, of course. No need to say anything. But if you'll do me a favor and just keep an eye out until we get our, well, our friend here upstairs."

Beaufort sighed heavily. "Of course, sir."

They headed up the stairs and had just reached the landing when they heard Beaufort speak in too loud a voice.

"Yes, your lordship, how may I assist you?"

The trio froze and scuttled to one side.

"Have you seen my blasted son?" a gruff voice bellowed below them. "I've been looking all over for him."

"Damn," said Bishop. "The pater!"

"Yes, your lordship," said Beaufort flatly. He gave a noncommittal wave towards the staircase. "He's just there, my lord."

"Damnit, Beaufort!" Bishop cursed under his breath.

With a shove, Bishop pushed Monty and the selkie into a small alcove which housed the servant's door for this level.

"I say, Bishop, is that you?"

Lord Brookesbay approached the bottom of the stairs.

"Yes, Father," Bishop called back.

"Where are you off to in such a rush?" his father asked.

Monty, overcome with nerves, pressed himself farther back into the alcove and without thinking he grabbed onto the blanket and pulled the selkie closer to him. His one thought was that they must be as flat as possible within the alcove to avoid being seen. Only after he had grabbed the man did he realize what he had done. The selkie was giving him a rather interesting look, and a smile graced his full lips.

The selkie shifted himself in such a way that the blanket began to fall from his shoulders, but Monty caught it up and lifted it back up.

"Must keep that on for now," he whispered.

The selkie raised an eyebrow and then spread his arm a bit, opening the blanket. Monty willed himself not to lance down and take in the full glory of the man's form. He could not in any fashion deny the seductiveness of the man, but it made him suspicious. The selkie extended his arms, wrapping Monty up in the blanket with him and pressing in so that they were as close as possible. The selkie rested his hands on Monty's waist, and Monty couldn't help but inhale of him. A deep scent, salty and savory, like something from the sea, and unmistakably masculine. He felt his body respond quite too readily, and he closed his eyes, willing his concentration elsewhere.

"I'm just off upstairs to assist Monty," he heard Bishop saying.

"What's wrong with the boy?" asked his father.

"Nothing wrong as such," Bishop extemporized. "It's just that he seems to have torn the sleeve of his best shirt while we were... playing, uh... croquet."

Even behind his closed lids, Monty couldn't help but roll his eyes at that.

"Damnable sport," chided Bishop's father. "Never saw the appeal myself."

"No, sir," answered Bishop.

"Well, once you've settled that, go see your mother. She has something important, it seems, to ask you about dinner. Something about a seating chart or a Charlotte Russe cake or some such."

"Yes, sir, I will," Bishop replied, at somewhat of a loss.

"Good, good," his father muttered and was off.

Monty opened his eyes and found the selkie's face close to his eyes. The man leaned in closer, his his mouth slightly open. A churning anxiety swept over Monty and he held his hand up, placing two fingers on the selkie's lips.

"No," he whispered fiercely.

A hurt expression flashed across the selkie's face, and, for a brief moment, Monty felt a certain sense of guilt. But, again, suspicion won over and he was glad he had not succumbed to the man's abundant charms quite so soon. *So soon,* he repeated in his mind. Which suggested that the event would inevitably repeat itself.

Just then Bishop appeared outside their cubbyhole.

"I say, chaps," Bishop said. "Time enough for that later. Let's get to my room."

Monty nodded as he gently pushed the selkie away from him.

Once inside the bedchamber, they both breathed a little easier and fell into postures of relaxation. Their new friend however was bright-eyed and alert and gazing around him, fascinated by all the ornate, over-gilded, and, frankly, in Monty's opinion, bad taste with which Bishop's room had been done up.

He let the driving blanket fall to his feet as he wandered about the room, studying the objects. He was extremely well-formed, more muscular than the average chap Monty had seen. But his muscles were long and lean, giving him a lithe grace. His skin was deep golden brown in color and glowed in the sunlight. His chest, and other regions of note, were covered in a dark, fine down that swirled around his large brown nipples, and highlighted the curve of his perfect arse. He was taller than even Bishop, it appeared, whom Monty considered unusually tall, and his head was topped with curly hair so dark brown as to look black, a lock of which fell down over his forehead and almost reached his eyes, which were framed by a squarish face containing a wide button nose and full, pouty lips.

As Monty watched him stride about the room, he thought of his days in the galleries in Paris. He had spent his days in France wandering all the many galleries and private shows as well as locked in the studio, with one wild-haired master or another, learning technique. He had discovered one particular artist who was the talk of all Paris ,and soon became fascinated with his work. An enormous sculpture by the artist had been installed in front of the *Panthéon* while they were in Paris called *The Thinker*. Monty had been drawn to return again and again to the piece, spending many hours standing across from it, either with pencil and paper in hand, or just silently studying it, learning its lines and proportions.

Usually, he could close his eyes and see those lines and shapes burned into his mind. But, now, as he closed his eyes and thought of those days, all he saw in his mind's eye was the image of the remarkable man sauntering mere feet from him.

"What shall we call him?" asked Bishop.

"I'm sorry, what?" Monty's eyes popped open.

"Well, we can't bloody well keep calling him *Him*. It's bound to cause confusion. Too many male pronouns often do."

Monty stared at the selkie.

"Rodin," he blurted out.

"More with the French, Monty?" Bishop grimaced, clearly exasperated. "It's a virtual obsession with you today."

Monty shrugged. "Well, he has a European air about him. And he reminds me of something."

The selkie smiled. "Rodin," he repeated.

The two friends exchanged a look of shock.

"Good lord," said Bishop. "The bloody creature is learning to speak."

Rodin nodded.

"I believe he seems to like it," said Monty.

"Rodin," repeated Rodin.

"After all, if people think he's French," added Monty. "It will help to explain his... oddity."

Bishop sighed and shrugged. "Yes, I suppose so. We ought to get the chap some clothing. He can't stand around here naked all day."

"Quite," said Monty.

"He's more my height, but possibly more your build up top. It may be a piecemeal effort, but I suppose we can make it work. I'll rummage through the closet here and maybe you can bring something from your room."

"Of course," said Monty, glad for something practical to do, and headed towards the door. "Shan't be a tick."

Rodin made to follow him. Monty stopped at the doorway.

"I say," cried Bishop, grabbing Rodin by the arm. "You ought to stay here, old man. Can't have you roaming the halls in the altogether, what."

Rodin let Bishop guide him back into the room.

"Monty," Rodin offered. "*Shan be a vick.*"

"I say, you're a quick study, aren't you," said Bishop. "Now if you wouldn't mind just staying still."

For some inexplicable reason, hearing his name on the lips of the selkie made Monty go all hot in the face, and he hurried out of the room before his blushing could be detected. As he moved down the hallway, he felt the heat spreading throughout his body. He shook his hands as he walked hoping to disperse it before it consumed him.

Chapter Four

Le Mans, France, 1906

"Blast," Monty exclaimed. He slapped the pencil down in the spine of his sketchbook and leaned back against the tree he sat under.

This heat was insufferable. Monty didn't usually mind a very warm day but this was too much. He had only traveled to this provincial area because Bishop, ever steeped in his fascination with the automobile, had secured an invitation to the *Grand Prix de l'Automobile Club de France*. Monty had managed most of the morning feigning interest in the racing cars going round and round like metal chariots in some weird absinthe fantasy until he could stand it no longer. He abandoned his friend to find some shade, any slice of relief from the pounding sun, and as he left he heard one of the attendees telling his friends the tarmac they had laid for the race had become so overheated it was softening and that the tyres of the cars might get stuck.

Pitiable souls they would be, in their tin cans, sweltering under the sun. And more pitiable the fools standing around watching them.

He had tried to read but found his concentration lacking, so pulled out his sketchbook. But that was now, as it had been for some weeks, a source of frustration for him. At times, and seemingly out of the blue, the only thing he could manage to draw were figures of a faceless man. Try as he might during these spells, he seemed unable to fashion anything more. They were flashes of obsession with this particular form, but on a day like today, they provided no mental quiet as sketching usually did for him.

He laid the sketchbook, open to clean pages, over his eyes and hoped sleep would arrive to distract him from the swelter. Success attained, he was awoken some time later by the tapping of a cane against the sole of his shoe. He raised his eyes to see a very handsome gentleman, clearly of some esteem judging by his wardrobe, standing above him. For a moment neither of them spoke; the man, maybe a decade his senior, rubbed his distinguished-looking moustache as he studied Monty.

"My name is Trevor," he said finally.

"Monty."

Trevor pointed with his cane at the copy of *Salome* lying beside Monty in the grass.

"You know," he said, "that was originally written in French."

"As is this edition," answered Monty.

"So you read French?"

"Better than I speak it, I'm afraid. If I'm to be honest, I was rather more entranced by the illustrations."

"An Englishman who actually makes an effort to learn French before visiting France. You surprise me."

"And how did you know—watching me sleep—that I was an Englishman?" asked Monty coyly.

Trevor gave a small smile that lifted his moustache, his eyes twinkling. "I took my chances." He waved his cane at the spot of shade next to Monty. "Do you mind if I join you?"

"Not at all."

As Trevor settled down beside him, Monty asked, "Have you read much Wilde?"

"Not really. I saw the *Earnest* play when I was younger. Entertaining for what it was, I suppose. Theatre isn't particularly my thing. And, of course, after that whole scandal of his imprisonment, one had to avoid his works. To make sure that the public didn't think too poorly of you, if you catch my meaning."

Monty lifted his chi.

"In my experience, the public never thinks much at all."

Trevor studied his face, his eyes lingering on his lips, Monty noticed.

"Easier said in Paris than back home," said Trevor.

"Easier said anywhere in the world—if you believe it," replied Monty.

"Quite."

Though he knew it was an absurd notion, as they had met only moments before and they were, of course, in public where such things could not happen, Monty in that moment had longed for Trevor to lean forward and kiss him. Perhaps it was the heat of the day; perhaps it was the headiness of being away from England, here in the picturesque surrounds of Le Mans, which made him feel so un-inhibited. What exactly he could not say, but later, looking back at that moment, he knew that some direct line to romance had opened up within Monty as concerned Trevor.

He had had his boyish pashes throughout the years, but when he met Trevor, something had changed within him—he had opened up to a new kind of attachment, something all the more adult, and all the more serious, with all the more threat of devastating consequence.

"This heat is intolerable," Trevor noted. "You are smart to hide under a tree."

"Anything to get away from those roaring tin box-es. Oh, I'm sorry. Do you very much like cars? I suppose you must if you're here."

"Well, you're here and certainly don't seem to care for them."

Monty smiled at being caught out.

"No," said Trevor. "I have business interests here, of a sort. But mainly I am here for my father's sake. He is rather passionate about automobiles and he demanded I attend to relay the details to him back home. Firsthand account and all that."

"If you're lazing under a tree with me, won't you miss all the details?"

Trevor ran his thumb and forefinger over his moustache, smoothing it down.

"I'm rather like my father in that way, you see. When I find something that drives my passion, all else becomes irrelevant."

"Indeed," Monty replied softly.

Trevor's eyes suddenly brightened.

"Have you seen the river yet?" he asked enthusiastically. "The Sarthe. It's not a far walk from here."

"No, I haven't."

Trevor got to his feet and offered Monty his hand. "Shall we go then? I imagine it's much cooler and more pleasant there away from all this noise and dust."

Monty grabbed the gloved hand and pulled himself to his feet. "Sounds delightful. I like anything to do with a river, or the sea, or water really."

He bent down to retrieve his books but Trevor beat him to it. "I'll carry those."

Monty wanted to protest but he had never had such caring attention paid to him by a man, so he did not.

"And your friend won't mind?" asked Trevor.

"My friend?"

"The ginger-haired one, who is so passionately devoted to the race. You arrived together so I assume you were meant to be spending the day together."

"You don't miss much, do you?" asked Monty, blushing a bit. "Bishop won't mind. Unless you suddenly sprang wheels for feet and began to trundle all over, he wouldn't notice my absence, I assure you."

"Then I shall endeavor to retain my ankles."

As they walked towards the river, a breeze came up and Monty's sketchbook fluttered open. Trevor clamped onto it so as not to drop it and gazed on the now open pages before closing it.

"Whoever your model was for these drawings, he certainly had an impressive form."

"There was no model. It's simply something I imagined."

"Indeed. Well, you have quite the healthy imagination. That one just under my thumb, he looks as if his legs are merging together. Like a mermaid or some sort of mer-person, I imagine."

"When I was a small child, do you know, my favorite book was Andersen's *Fairy Tales* and I always made my amah read me the story about the mermaid?"

"And now you've graduated to *Salome*."

"I think *The Little Mermaid* is still much more my style."

"Perhaps I ought not to take you to the river. You aren't suddenly going to sprout gills and swim away from me, are you?"

Monty smiled at him. "We'll just have to see, I suppose."

Trevor was right, and once they reached the riverbank, the heat had diffused quite some bit. But the sun still shone bright ,and Monty itched for relief.

"Come, let's have a swim," Monty declared.

"A swim? We can't bathe in the river."

"Why not?"

"For one thing, I'm sure it's illegal somehow. And, too, there." He pointed across the river. "There's a whole village of factories just there. What if some-one sees us?"

"It's France," Monty said. "They don't mind such things."

"Don't they?"

"Besides, you're a very handsome man. If they see anything at all, I'm sure it will be a delightful sight."

Trevor smiled and Monty saw the blush on his cheeks.

"I certainly don't compare with that man in your sketches."

"That is solely a man of my creation—a sort of mythical man," replied Monty as he shucked off his jacket. "While you're a very real man. So I wouldn't think there would be need to compare. Besides, why would you need to worry how you compare?"

He tossed down his waistcoat and began to unbut-ton his shirt.

"If I intend to keep your attention for more than just this one afternoon, I should concern myself with how appealing I am. Shouldn't I?"

"Likely you should," agreed Monty.

He tossed his shirt onto the pile of clothes de-veloping on the ground and peeled off his under-shirt, so that he stood there stripped to the waist. Trevor's eyes moved over his exposed skin, drinking in every inch. Monty had never had a man look at him like that, slowly, longingly. He felt admired and acclaimed. It made him feel powerful.

He stepped forward and moved in close to Trevor.

"The heat is unbearable. You know you want to."

Monty began to unbutton his trousers, sliding them down to the ground. It had been too hot for a union suit or any undergarments that day, so he stood there, nude and ready for the water. Trevor could not control his gaze as he too began to disrobe. Monty smiled at him and then turned and ran towards the river, jumping in with a loud howl, and splashing hard into the water.

It was pure bliss. The silkiness of the waves touching every part of his body. He swam to the surface and held his face to the sun to let it be warmed and then dove back down, seeking the cool darkness below. Trevor gave a small yelp at the temperature, but was soon swimming and diving with as much fervor as Monty. They splashed one another and swam in differing formations as if in a chase.

Monty got so lost in the feeling that he began to ignore Trevor, diving deeper and deeper down towards the bottom of the river. Each descent, his lungs stretched to their maximum, thrilled him. On one of his dives he felt something bump against him down below. It was too murky to make out exactly, and Trevor swam away too fast for him to bump him back. He headed for the surface and looked around to find Trevor treading water almost three yards from him.

"You're fast," cried Monty.

"What do you mean?" asked Trevor.

"How did you bump me down below and then swim that far out so quickly?"

Trevor shook his head in delightful confusion. "But I didn't bump you. I've been here for the last several minutes."

Monty cut his eye at him.

"Whatever you say. I don't mind games in the least."

And with that he sprang up from the water in a small dive and came crashing on the surface, splashing Trevor mightily. Underneath, Monty swam down and down again just as before. And just as before, he felt a bump against his legs. He zoomed to the surface, gasping and smiling, and looking for Trevor. But his new friend was on the banks of the river, basking in the sun.

"You did it again," cried Monty as he swam to him. "You bumped me below."

Trevor studied his body as he emerged from the water.

"I assure you I did not. I would save that type of behavior for somewhere far more private."

"Then who was it?" asked Monty as he lay down beside Trevor in the grass.

"Or maybe what was it?" Trevor offered with a raised brow. "Possibly there are creatures living in the river. Or maybe you've awakened one of your mermaid friends, after all."

Monty laughed. "If only."

They lay there in the sun, drying and sunning themselves, eyes closed.

"Are you staying in Paris?" Monty asked, without opening his eyes.

"Of course," replied Trevor. "I've seen you around, you know."

"Have you?"

"Of course. Boys as beautiful as you don't go unnoticed."

Monty didn't reply, only smiled.

"Your friend. The one you're always with. Is he your lover?"

"Bishop? God no."

"That was a very quick answer. Almost too quick. Are you quite sure?"

"Answered quickly because it is definitive. Bishop and are more like brothers than anything. I care for him as if he were my own blood, very deeply, but not at all in that way."

"That's good news then," said Trevor, his voice heavy.

"It is?"

Monty opened his eyes and rolled on to his side to find Trevor studying him.

"Oh, yes. Very good news indeed."

After their swim, they headed back to the racetrack, hopeful the festivities had waned and a train ride back to the city awaited them. As they approached the track, Trevor lifted his cane to point.

"It looks as if your companion has a new acquaintance," he said.

"Bishop always has a new acquaintance. He collects them like ha'pennies."

Monty followed the length of Trevor's cane and saw Bishop with a large, older man. As if he sensed he was being watched, the man turned and stared directly at Monty. Suddenly Monty felt queer all over. Making eye contact with the man, something inside him just vibrated, like a large bell. It wasn't fear exactly, at least he didn't think so, but an extreme wariness, like an instinct to flee. He felt as if he were a creature of the wild about to come to battle with a territorial neighboring beast. What an odd impression from just a look, and it troubled him.

"Who is that?" he said, hoping his emotion did show through.

"I've seen him in the city as well," said Trevor. "Always stalking about the younger men. Queer fellow, to be honest. German or Austrian or something like that, I forget.

As they came closer, the intensity of the man's gaze seemed to soften, and by the time they had reached Bishop, the man appeared as normal and benign as anyone.

"Ah, Monty, there you are," said Bishop. "I thought you'd scarpered back to Paris."

"No, no," said Monty. "Not as far as all that. Just down to the river. To take in the cooler air."

Bishop glanced from Monty to Trevor and nodded.

"Yes, of course. The cooler air."

Monty opened his mouth to make introductions but realized he only had Trevor's Christian name.

"Good afternoon, Lord Brookesbay, nice to meet you," said Trevor. "I'm Trevor Portland-Kirby, Lord Mawnton."

"Pleased to meet you," said Bishop. "I feel silly for you knowing me and me not knowing you."

"I know you by reputation only. Though I believe our brothers did something together at one school or another."

"Indeed. Sounds very likely," said Bishop. "May I introduce Herr Aufhocker: Lord Mawnton, as you've heard, and this is my friend Mister Singer."

"*Na, guten tag*," Herr Aufhocker said gruffly with a nod.

"Uncle Freddy has been telling me all about cars today. He is a manufacturer, you know, back in his country."

"Pardon. Who has been telling you?"

Bishop chuckled. "I apologize. Herr Aufhocker—Friedrich. We've gotten so close already, I've decided to call him Uncle Freddy."

"Yes. I see," said Monty. But something stirred within him and he worried about his friend's new acquaintance, despite the cuddly name.

Monty glanced at "Uncle Freddy" who seemed to be studying Monty. Something about the way Uncle Freddy—no, he couldn't think of him like that—something about the way *Friedrich* looked at him made his skin crawl. Friedrich brought his hand up to his chin as he gave Monty a thorough on-ceover, and Monty noticed he wore a bracelet. It resembled a linked chain, and its color was like copper that had built up a patina. A mixture of green and bronze overlay the reddish brown metal beneath, and, in the center of the chain, hung something like a charm. It was fashioned in the shape of a circle with a large dot in the middle. Monty had seen the symbol before, but its meaning he could not remember.

"It looks like we've all made new friends today," said Bishop cheerfully. "And you said you never wanted to come, Monty. I bet you don't regret it now."

Monty wasn't sure if he did or not. "If we catch the next train, we can be back in Paris for dinner," said Bishop. "Maybe we can all break bread together? With a bottle or two of *vin ordinaire*, of course."

"That sounds splendid," replied Trevor.

Monty glanced at "Uncle Freddy" and they made eye contact. That vibration rumbled through him again, and he swore he could sense quite an intensity coming from his gaze. And then suddenly he smiled and nodded, the mask disappearing.

Monty turned away and walked in the direction of the train station with the others, a cold feeling in the pit of his stomach.

Chapter Five

London, 1910

Monty and Rodin stood on the sidewalk, waiting for Bishop to secure his automobile. Monty felt glad to be back in London and peered around, taking it all in.

Large double-decker buses passed by on the street, the fronts of their chassis looking very much like Bishop's auto, with advertisement placards on their top levels reading *Pears—The Soap Kings* and *Veno's Lightning Cough Cure*. On one, a young man dangled carelessly from the staircase at the rear and waved at Monty shouting, "Good afternoon, guv!" A horse-drawn trolley ambled past behind, on its dark awning in bright white letters, *Midland Railway—White Cross St*. There were hawkers at the corners selling newspapers, apples, and jellied eels, all seemingly in competition to see who could bellow the loudest. The rag-and-bone man galumphed down the other side of the avenue, pushing his precariously balanced cart of dusty and dirty goods, his shoes stuffed with newsprint.

It was loud and dirty and thrilling.

Rodin peered in every direction, wide-eyed and possibly overwhelmed. Standing there, in his trousers inches too short, his ankles exposed, and his shoulders straining the fabric of his jacket, almost like a young boy whose mother had abandoned him in the middle of a fairground. That Bishop had tried to squeeze his tweed caps onto the man didn't help, and it popped up, perched on his thick curls, and tilted rakishly over his forehead. The image tugged at his heart, despite his resistance, and the side of his mouth curled up in a smile. He turned back the garage, wondering what was taking Bishop so long.

It was hard to believe that not far from here at all, Monty's parents were snuggled away in their well-kept terraced house. Their quiet neighborhood full of respectable middle-class people strolling leisurely, passing nannies with their charges and well-dressed women in pairs, all peering out grandly over the green park that ran alongside. It was only minutes away in a hansom cab but it might have been another world entirely. This was the London that gave Monty energy, that kept him coming back no matter where he travelled, and, for all its comfort and repose, the world of his parents felt like something akin to death to him. It was a suffocating place and, though he cared a great deal for his family, he avoided it as much as he could. He only hoped he did not run into his sister while in the city, as he knew she would chastise him for not yet visiting, her words saying one thing but her inference being the shame he ought to feel for not doing what was expected of him.

"Here we are then, chaps," cried Bishop as he bounded out of the doors. "Shall we fetch a hansom cab then?"

Seeing the two well-dressed men standing there with their luggage, despite their oddly attired friend, a cabbie soon came to a stop.

"Isn't it a bit ridiculous," said Monty as they climbed into the cab, "to have to take a cab to and from your automobile?"

Rodin leant him a hand and pulled him onto the seat beside him, where they both faced Bishop.

"Rather defeats the purpose, doesn't it?" Monty added.

"It's a garage and it's the only one with a charging station near the house. I'll pick her up tomorrow and she'll be like new, ready to go again."

There was a loud *thud* and the carriage shook on its leather strappings.

"And why that enormous trunk?" asked Monty as he tried to settle himself. "I thought we were only coming for a night or two to look for Weaver. You've packed as if we might soon catch the transatlantic and flee for Argentina."

"You really are like a maiden aunt today aren't you, Monty? Don't be so tiresome."

"Tarsome," echoed Rodin.

Monty cut his eye at the short-trousered fellow.

"You see," Bishop said with a nod. "Even our exotic friend agrees."

"But what is the purpose of so large a trunk for so short a trip?"

"I don't know how short the trip shall be. I shall let caprice carry me as always. And it's only my quick travel trunk, besides."

"'Travel trunk'? That enormous thing?"

"Yes, my valet keeps it packed on the occasion I may need to suddenly dash off somewhere. Just the essentials. For eventualities."

"I can't imagine anyone would get anything quickly moving that mammoth thing other than a hernia. Of course, once your parents find out we have invaded their London townhouse, we may need to stay there for quite some time, I grant you."

"They'll never know, and wouldn't object besides. They hardly ever use the place these days except when I make trips into the city. Father is so obsessed with the racing at Newmarket, he rarely leaves the area except in winter. And then, of course, he says, who wants to spend the winter in London?"

"We will be able to manage? Since it's been shut up and, though I think my domestic skills do exceed yours, even I can't light a boiler."

"Not to worry, my fraught little maiden aunt," said Bishop. "Mama always keeps a small staff in residence for eventualities and to keep the place in good nick. In fact, the cook there, still just an assistant yet, exceeds Mrs. Shipley at the manor, though we'd never say, of course."

"Of course," added Rodin with a smile.

"This one may be far too clever for his own good, Monty. You'd better watch out."

Monty looked at Rodin who smiled back at him, and put his arm against the back of the seating bench so that it draped over Monty's shoulders. Monty shifted, pushing the arm back into Rodin's lap.

"I don't think we're quite there yet, sir," Monty chided.

Rodin seemed slightly miffed but offered no argument.

"Oh, Monty," sighed Bishop.

"What have I done to exasperate you now?" asked Monty, brow raised.

"Nothing at all. Only I do wish you let yourself be more open to joy."

Monty crossed his legs and tugged at his waistcoat.

"That isn't in the style of the maiden aunt though, is it?" Monty glanced out of the window. "It's late afternoon already. The usual crowd won't be pouring in to the Brunswick until well after dark. Do you think we ought to try calling on the Weaver before then?"

"Do you know where he stays in London?"

"No, of course not. I only assumed you did. Since you seem to have history together."

Bishop narrowed his eyes at Monty. "Well, dear Aunt, I'm afraid I haven't the foggiest clue. We've only ever met at the Brunswick or at our gentleman's club. But I'm told the Weaver's appearances there are quite rare."

"'Weaver'?" Rodin asked.

"Yes," said Monty flatly. "He's going to tell us what exactly to do with you. And speaking of weaving, we'll need to find this one appropriate clothing before we parade him about the city. Any chance your tailor is available?"

"Not this late in the day. But I'm sure there are some of the Pater's old suits at the townhouse. He always keeps something there, just in case."

"Of eventualities?"

"Like Pater, like progeny. Ah, here we are."

As the cab came to a stop, Bishop leapt out and stood on the sidewalk briefly before prancing to the foot of the front steps. He stretched his arms and inhaled deeply.

"Oh, how I have missed the city!" he exclaimed.

"Not to worry, Bishop," Monty said dryly, paying the cabbie. "We can manage the luggage."

"Oh, leave it," Bishop answered. "I'll send one of the boys down for it."

He galloped up the stairs and Monty followed.

"Are the staff having a party?" he asked, pointing to the nearby window.

Shadows seemed to be moving behind the drapes and they could hear a waltz being played on the piano.

"Well done them if so," said Bishop heartily.

He pressed the bell ring beside the door.

"Electric bell system now too, we've got," said Bishop. "Damned fine thing. The London house has all the up-to-dates, thankfully."

After a few moments, the large doors slowly opened to reveal a wizened old goat of a man, half stooped by age. Despite his years and stature, his livery was fresh and crisply pressed and his hair oiled into a neat shape. He stared at them with a solemn expression.

"Good god, Davies!" exclaimed Bishop.

"Good evening, sir," the butler replied.

"But you're still alive then," said Bishop.

"Only just, sir."

"Splendid. Well, my friends and I—you remember Monty, don't you?"

"Of course. Good evening, Mister Singer."

"Good evening, Mister Davies," replied Monty.

"We'll be staying for a couple of nights, or possibly longer," Bishop continued.

"Yes, sir."

"Is there someone about who might help with our bags?"

"I shouldn't think they need attending, sir," replied Davies, lifting his chin.

Bishop and Monty turned around to see Rodin stood behind them with the large trunk under one arm like a mere trifle, along with the other bags they had brought.

"Oh my," muttered Monty breathily.

"I say, well done," said Bishop. "Here, step aside, Monty. Put them just there in the foyer if you don't mind, Rodin."

Rodin moved into the house to deposit the bags and they followed. The music they had heard from outside was even louder now.

"Is there some sort of celebration happening this evening, Davies?" asked Bishop.

Davies turned to press a bell to summon footmen for dealing with the luggage.

"Of a sort, my lord. Lady Denglarry is in residence presently."

Bishop and Monty exchanged a surprised look.

"Aunt Charlotte?" exclaimed Bishop. "Good lord."

"The Lord is often called upon when my name is mentioned," said a mellifluous voice which floated into the hall

They turned to see the sister of Bishop's father, Charlotte Parthemore, Marchioness of Denglarry, moving toward them. The family resemblance was always i evident, but where in Bishop it gave him an orangey ginger coloring, his aunt's hair was doused in a fiery red that set her green eyes to sparkle. They were made all the more lively by a sumptuous gown of emerald hue, and jewels to match.

"Has your mother sent you all this way to chide me?" she asked as she got close.

"Chide you?" asked Bishop.

"Yes, I sent word earlier today. It was terrible of me, but I simply had to cancel my invitation to dinner. I assume she was livid to have her numbers thrown off like that."

"That must have been what Father was talking about," replied Bishop, realization dawning. "Aunt Charlotte, not a Charlotte Russe cake."

"And now she has sent my favorite nephew to scold me properly. I do cherish dear Elizabeth, but I had to disappoint her. I couldn't abide another one of her dreary affairs—they're all soft piano and syllabub and I simply droop from exhaustion thinking of it."

In the background, three young men, presumably footmen, had appeared and carried off the luggage as Davies followed them.

"Then she will be even more upset since we have also absconded and left her at an even odder seating," added Monty.

"Dear, Monty," cried Charlotte. "Come here, my dear, handsome boy, how long it has been since I've seen you?"

She pulled his face close and kissed him on either cheek.

"You always were my favorite of Bishop's friends," she said. "And the most handsome."

"Thank you, Lady Denglarry." Monty felt his cheeks flush at the attention.

"Oh, pish, none of that. You must call me Aunt Charlotte as well. You're practically a brother to dear Bishop anyway." She directed her attention to Rodin. "And who, pray tell, is your magnificent companion?"

"A new friend of ours," hastened Monty. "His name is Rodin."

"He's from Spain," interjected Bishop. "So his English is very limited."

Monty gave Bishop a pointed look. "France. He's from France actually."

"Ah," said Lady Denglarry as she extended her hand. "*J'ai toujours aimé un Français.*"

Rodin took her hand and kissed it delicately.

"*Vous me flattez, madame,*" Rodin said. "*Enchanté.*"

Monty and Bishop exchanged bemused glances.

"You must all join me," she declared. "I am expecting some guests this evening for a little amusement of cards and champagne and whatever else we devise."

She gave Rodin a coquettish smile.

"We would love to, Aunt," Bishop said. "Only we've promised Monsieur Rodin that we would take him to meet a few friends of interest tonight in the city."

"You just wish to keep him all to yourselves, I see," she said, giving Monty a wink. "And I can't blame you. But surely one drink before you go, I would love for him to meet my friends. And his English won't be a problem, I'm sure he'll be able to find someone to chat to in French."

Monty raised his brows. "Apparently so."

Rodin smiled in reply.

"Then it's settled," said Aunt Charlotte.

"What's settled, darling?"

They all turned in the direction of the booming male voice that rang across the foyer. There stood a very tall, square-jawed gentleman with a moustache. He surveyed their little scene with a broad smile on his face, studying each of them openly.

"Oh, Anderson, dear," cried Aunt Charlotte. "Do come and meet everyone."

The mustachioed gentleman sauntered over in his evening dress, and as he approached, Monty noticed he was almost as tall as Rodin.

"Everyone this is my friend, Mister Anderson Herald. He's an American."

"By no fault of my own," added Anderson with a laugh.

Introductions were made, and Aunt Charlotte continued.

"We were discussing the boys joining us for this evening's frolics, but they do insist on their own plans. However, I have convinced them to stay for at least one drink to meet our friends. I think they would just adore them, and Monsieur Rodin here has only just arrived and so deserves a proper welcoming. Wouldn't you say?"

Anderson gave Rodin a thorough once-over. "Yes, of course."

"Yes, you see, the thing is," Monty began, "that our friend here has lost his luggage during his travels and is in need of a decent change of clothes."

"I noticed those trousers were awfully high at the bottom and tight at the center," agreed Anderson.

Bishop raised a brow.

"He looks about your size doesn't he, darling?" offered Aunt Charlotte. "Could you spare something?"

"Yes, just for a day or so," said Monty. "Until we can get him to the tailor tomorrow."

"Happy to help," nodded Anderson. "That's what I like to see, a good solid fellow. A man with meat on his bones." He reached out to grab Rodin's arm playfully. "Good Lord, it's like a steel barrel under there. You're not a joke, are you, son?"

"Yes, isn't he magnificent?" said Charlotte. "And you're almost the same height so I don't think the hems will be any trouble. I'm sure we have a nimble-fingered maid who could take things in around the waist rather quickly."

"Hey, now," objected Anderson.

"I'm sure Davies will sort it all out," continued Charlotte.

"Of course, ma'am," said Davies from behind them.

Bishop jumped. "Good lord, old man, have you been there this whole time? I thought you'd left."

"Like the poor, sir, I am always there," answered Davies. "Shall I fetch any particular suit from your room, sir?"

"Any of them will do," said Anderson. "Have at them."

Davies nodded.

"We'll handle the cufflinks and all that," added Monty.

"Yes, sir," said Davies as he shuffled off.

"Splendid," said Charlotte, quite pleased.

"Well, I expect we had better get—" began Bishop.

"Where did you say you were from again?" asked Anderson of Rodin.

Monty gave Bishop a warning glance.

"I spent some time in Brazil, you know," continued Anderson, "And you remind me of those fellows I met down there. Solid, good-looking people they have. *Você fala português*?"

"*Sim senhor. Eu faço*," answered Rodin without hesitation.

Anderson guffawed as Monty and Bishop looked at one another slack-jawed.

"Well, that beats the Dutch!" said Anderson. "*E voce e do Brasil*?"

"*Eu sou de muitos lugares*," said Rodin with a small shrug of the shoulders. He glanced over at Monty. "I go only where I want."

Monty experienced an odd feeling at that statement, as if it were meant just for him. The sentiment crept over him again that somehow Rodin was as familiar to him as an old friend. But, of course, that couldn't be. Why did this man insist on invoking such suspicion on Monty's part?

"Quite," said Bishop, clearing his throat. "Yes, well, we'd better get upstairs to freshen up a bit before changing for the evening. Been on the road all day, and it might be a late night for us."

They began to move toward the stairwell in the center of the great hall.

"Did you come in here in that great contraption of yours?" asked Charlotte.

"I have a new automobile now, actually," Bishop replied.

"It's a Baker Electric," offered Monty all too sweetly, smiling at Bishop's piercing expression.

"Such astonishing gadgets my nephew is taken with," said Charlotte. "Do they have those in America, dear Anderson? These electric coaches?"

"Not for long if we can help," said Anderson manfully.

Bishop paused at the stairwell. "And why is that?"

"Coal's where it's at, son. Gasoline. None of this fussy electric stuff. You've got to have big power for these new machines."

"Indeed. Well, Americans have always had rather an obsession with power, haven't they? We shall join you soon, Aunt."

"Yes, do," said Charlotte as she guided Anderson back towards the drawing room. "Our guests will be arriving within the next few hours."

They headed up the stairs and Monty glanced back to make sure they were out of earshot.

"Spain, by the way?" he said. "I thought we agreed he was from France?"

"Not to worry, no one like my aunt will know the difference. Besides, as our friend has proven to be a librarian in the Tower of Babel, I suspect it hardly matters."

"Yes," said Monty emphatically, coming to a stop at the top of the stairs. He turned to Rodin. "What was that all about? Only hours ago you could barely speak, so it seemed, and now you are some sort of living translation device."

Rodin dipped his head and looked at Monty through his lashes.

"*L'anglais,*" Rodin said, "*est un travail difficile pour la langue.*"

Bishop gave them a sly look. "Not for long, one imagines."

"I'm sure I don't know what you mean," declared Monty, though even he was unsure to which man he was responding.

Bishop moved down the hallway and waved his hand to left of the corridor.

"Here is my room. And I assume the two of you will be quite happy in these two rooms just across. Davies always arranges things so competently, so I'm sure they've been aired and are ready—what with Aunt Charlotte's guests on the way. If her usual crowd is any indication, there may be many overnight guests. Still, there's plenty of rooms. Oh, but that is," he said, turning to Monty and Rodin with a playful look, "unless you'd prefer to share?"

Monty ignored this. "Are we sure neither of these rooms are spoken for by your aunt herself?"

"Oh, no. She's sure to be in the master suite of rooms that Mamma and the Pater share."

"And Mister Anderson Herald?"

"The American can bed wherever he likes, as I understand is their custom."

"Your aunt does not seem very concerned about scandal, but is she not at all worried about your uncle finding out about her infamous parties?"

"The Most Honourable The Marquess of Denglarry? I should think not." Bishop scoffed. "No, Uncle and his dreadful son—my cousin Jasper if I must claim him—spend most of their time perfecting their *flânerie* around Venice and other assorted Mediterranean locales. Both have a propensity for Italian wine and Italian whores in the most unseemly of ways. Still, it leaves Aunt Charlotte to her own devices, which she much prefers, of course." A wistful expression flashed across Bishop's face. "Though the American was a rather handsome device, wasn't he? Despite his poor taste in automobiles."

"Do try and control yourself, Bishop," Monty said as he moved to examine the first room. "We can't have you seducing your aunt's favorite companion."

"I don't know that Aunt Charlotte has a favorite. Besides, I think he rather preferred our multi-tongued friend to either of us."

The suggestion stung Monty in a way he cared not to acknowledge, but still he glanced at Rodin nonetheless.

"I do not prefer the rather handsome device," Rodin said plainly.

"A man of his own tastes," declared Bishop.

Monty peered into the room whose door he had opened just moments before.

"Ah, yes, there's my case. So this is my room. I expect you're just next door then." He nodded to Rodin. "Yes, well, if you need anything, you know where we are. Once your new suit arrives, do give a bark if you need assistance."

"Monty, don't be so horrible," Bishop admonished as he slipped into his room, closing the door behind him.

Rodin stood in the hallway, not moving, and looking at Monty, his expression soft and studied. For some reason, Monty could not turn away or will his feet to move and they stood staring into one another's eyes. The light from the hallway sconces lit up the gold flecks in Rodin's brown eyes, and they seemed to sparkle. He reached over and grasped Monty's hand.

"Monty," he whispered.

That small touch sent a shimmer through Monty like an electrical current.

Monty blinked and turned away. He wanted to say something in reply but suddenly the sound of the sea rushed in his ears and he couldn't hear anything but the crashing of waves. He moved into the bedroom without speaking and the feeling of an invisible sea all around overcame him. The electricity continued to course through his body and he felt as if he might lift from the soft rug beneath him and float to the ceiling.

It was a feeling at once exhilarating and frightening.

Chapter Six

Paris, France, 1907

As the lazy *clop* of the horse hooves of the cab echoed on the cobblestones behind them, Monty shivered a bit, pulling his coat closer. What made him shiver was not the cooling air of the autumn night but rather the scene before him.

He gazed up at the cabaret entrance. The doorway façade was carved so that patrons would enter through the open jaws of a giant Leviathan, his large heavy-lidded eyes, wide and crazed, and his thick tongue winding its way along the bottom of the doorway. Around this enormous ghoul were stucco scenes of women being devoured by the flames of Hell.

"Can this really be the place?" asked Monty, gobsmacked.

"This is the address Bishop gave us," said Trevor.

"Yes, it is. But my god. Surely it must be this entrance beside," said Monty, fairly awestruck.

The smaller entrance which Monty indicated was just a few steps from the hellacious one and its façade was adorned with trumpeting angels.

"*Non, monsieur*," said a man standing by the less threatening doorway, as if on guard. "This is the exit only. You must go first through *L'Enfer* to leave through *Le Ciel*."

"How poetically French," said Trevor with a small snort. "Or is it Frenchly poetic?"

"You've been in Paris far longer than I," said Monty. "I'm surprised you've never been here before."

"I've heard of the *Cabaret du Néant*, which seems a similar effort, but I admit I never went. I thought it only did illusionist exhibitions and séances and that sort of thing. Naturally not my personal tastes."

"Naturally," agreed Monty.

"Besides, I am not much of one for cabarets in general. The amount of culture I have obtained this last year is solely due to your influence." He gave Monty with a wicked grin. "I should have known following you would eventually drag me to Hell."

"Au contraire, monsieur," Monty replied with a wink. "As the gentleman has just indicated, I will only take you to Heaven in the end."

"Promises, promises," said Trevor. "Now, shall we?"

He held out his hand towards the entrance to the *Cabaret de l'Enfer* so that Monty might precede him. As they reached the door, it was flung open and the impressive doorman, dressed in a Devil costume, boomed out, "Enter and be damned!"

"A touch dramatic," said Trevor, giving the doorman a once-over.

"I rather like it," said Monty with a smile.

"Of that I am not at all surprised." Trevor lifted his hand to indicate some of the artwork adorning the walls inside the cabaret. "After all, I did discover you nose-deep in such imagery when we first met."

"I don't think Aubrey Beardsley ever did anything so demonic, but I take your point."

Monty was still taking in the place and barely noticed any of the patrons. All of the walls were painted black and the art that was hung was also in black and white, not a stitch of color. The walls themselves were not smooth surfaces, rather they had all sorts of macabre and menacing masks, shapes, and scenes molded onto them—also painted black. There was a corridor of tables and booths and the ceiling hung over them, bowed and uneven, like the inside of a rocky cavern.

"Ah, here's your Pearl," said Trevor.

Monty turned where Trevor indicated and saw his friend Wu Zhenyi, whom everyone knew as Pearl. She was talking to one of the waitstaff who was dressed in yet another Devil-inspired costume.

They made their way over to her and exchanged greetings.

"I am glad to see you," said Monty. "Do you mean to tell me that Mister Loo set you free for an evening?"

"Of a fashion," replied Pearl. "He's here as well. You'll find him in the performance space with his lady friend, of course."

"Mister Loo?" asked Trevor. "That's the rather dandy gentleman I see all over the city?"

"Oui," answered Pearl. "*Alors il pense.*"

"When they are not working for Mister Zhang, Mister Loo has Pearl slaving away as he prepares to open his own art gallery and shop. I can't criticize the man's efforts too greatly since he did manage to sell a few of my pieces. Of course, he would never have even known about me if not for Pearl."

Pearl, in fact, had become invaluable to the art scene having emigrated from a Chinese enclave of Indochine and having French as her native tongue. She served as the liaison not only for Mister Zhang on many of his business efforts, but had smoothed many a transaction for the up-and-coming Mister Loo as well.

"He has come to hear Jade sing tonight," added Pearl.

"And has he ever come to support a showing of your own paintings?"

"Oui. But he does not approve of my paintings. *Mais enfin*, he does not approve of anything he cannot sell to an American. *Bizarre, n'est-ce pas?* Come, let me take you to the cabaret."

Pearl, like Monty, was here to support her best friend, Daiyu, who referred to herself as Jade. They were inseparable, but unlike Monty and Bishop, Monty had heard in the circles in which such things were talked about, they were also lovers.

Around the city, they were generally referred to as the Twin Jewels of the Orient. Of course, they weren't twins at all, and didn't even look alike. But the pair reveled in this joke, laughing at the names they had chosen for themselves, knowing the

Parisians didn't realize they were being made fun of.

But by night and on her days off, Pearl got to be her true self. A painter, an astonishing artist, who was smarter and more perceptive than most. When she wasn't painting, she socialized, embedding herself in the fabric of the city so that she could secure patrons and buyers for her work.

"There," she said as they entered the performance space at the back of the club. "He's just there with Madame Olga."

Pearl lifted her fingers in a small wave. Mister Loo nodded at her then the men, and Olga released the cigarette holder from her lips long enough to blow a halo of smoke, which she then dipped her head into. The jewels on her ears sparkled in the smoke and made Monty think of the fog rolling in over the Seine at night, reflecting the lights of the city.

"That woman," said Pearl softly, the smile still on her face, "*Très vulgaire.*"

The larger space they were in was much like the first, aesthetically. It was much more open with far more seating, but the overall shape of the room still suggested a cavern of sorts. The booths which lined the back walls, like the ones occupied by Loo and Madame Olga, were much more lavishly appointed than the former area of the cabaret, painted black, like everything else, but covered with plush cushions in a deep maroon color. The gas sconces on the walls were encased in red glass so that they shed a bloody patina on all they fell upon. The tables on the sunken floor a few steps down were covered in black cloths, and each one held a candle in the center, which burned from inside a red glass. There was a higher level, accessed by some staircase in the space, which served as a balcony of sorts. But, it too being painted in all black and dimly lit, seemed more a shelf of shadows hovering above them.

"They are certainly adamant in their theme," Monty said to Trevor who chuckled and nodded.

"So Bishop and Jade will be singing together then?" asked Trevor.

"Oui, oui," said Pearl. "I have heard them practicing and they are quite good. Their voices make a beautiful harmony."

"Yes, I must say," added Monty, "Bishop has always been a terrific singer, but he seems to have flourished beyond measure since we came to Paris."

"Perhaps it is the air here," said Pearl. "Paris infects one with romance."

"I must imagine they make a breathtaking couple together," said Trevor.

"Beautiful together, perhaps," said Pearl with a smile. "But neither of the type of beauty shared by the other."

"Quite."

"I have a table just up front for us," said Pearl.

On the small raised platform that served as a stage, there sat a cellist and violinist next to a small piano. The pianist emerged from the audience and sat down to a soft murmur of applause. The stage area was the only bit not lit with the garish red lighting, instead with two plain white spotlights. So that when Bishop and Jade emerged onto the stage from somewhere deeper in the back, they seemed almost angelic in contrast. They stood in the center of the stage and the audience settled to a hush.

Bishop practically radiated light standing there and Monty smiled with pride. Gone was the child-ishness that had softened Bishop's looks for so many years. His skin, as pale as eve, glowed with health and shone clear and smooth. His hair was like a crown of copper, framing his head with just the right waves and folds. Monty had never seen him more attrac-tive, and he again marveled at how much Bishop had come into his own in Paris.

He had always been handsome, and used the attention it provided much to his advantage. But the aura he resonated now was more than physical beauty, beyond aesthetics. He seemed to be lit from within, of late, with something almost akin to mag-ic.

Monty glanced at Trevor, his own handsome pro-file cutting against the darkness of the dimly lit space, and he felt satisfied. Paris seemed to have solidified life for both he and Bishop. Bishop had found a new calling in his pursuit of music, and Monty had found love, actual love, for the first time.

Trevor turned to him and smiled. He grabbed Monty's hand and squeezed his fingers.

The music began and Monty turned his full at-tention to it. The duo sang a couple of songs, alle-gro moderato in tempo, and their voices bounced playfully around one another. The arrangements were spring-like in their sunniness and the contrast, against this dark, hazy construction of a place felt almost surreal.

Bishop's voice ascended to heights Monty had never heard from him. His high notes jumped into octaves Monty was sure he had never visited before, and his tenor notes shimmered, dancing out into the air and enveloping the listener in what felt like a cocoon of silvered happiness. It was invigorating. Even Trevor, who always remained rather stoic when presented with any music, let his fingers thrum against the tabletop and his foot wag.

The crowd applauded vigorously after the second number as Bishop and Jade moved two small piano stools onto the stage and seated themselves.

"We should like to change the mood for a moment if you would allow us," said Bishop to the audience.

"Something for the heart," added Jade. Monty saw Pearl dip her head, a broad smile on her face.

A slim young man, dressed in all black, slipped up to their table, refilling their wine glasses, as the opening strains floated from the piano.

The song that proceeded was mesmerizing in its beauty. Monty could not place it though it reminded him somewhat of Elgar's *Romance* but as if it had been molded by Chopin.

On a night my love strode the banks, by the waters opal black

And talked to me of our hearts that might not ever be the same

It was a song, as Jade said, for the heart. But it was a heart that was broken. Bishop sang the bulk of the song, with Jade coming in for harmonies. And Monty was moved beyond measure. Something about how the soft yet pervasive the notes were felt as if a caress. They tickled his chest and caused his breath to catch.

A strange mixture of sorrow and sensuality overcame him. The song was like the soft fog of a hookah cloud or the hazy shift of drinking absinthe. The edges around him blurred and yet he felt more focused than ever. Every pluck of a piano key, every strain of the mournful cello, he could feel against his skin.

When Bishop sang the melody, Monty could feel it in the back of his throat. Like the catch before a sob, Bishop's voice at once carved him out and clutched the pieces of him together.

Worn most to cover up our shame
With hope that none would know our names

And in the atmosphere of all this, Monty wondered how Bishop could sing like this. The sunny, genial, pretty boy who seemed to bounce through life, never letting much of anything or anyone affect him. How could that young man know this type of depth; how could he communicate such sorrow and longing and regret? What could he know of such mournful love, of such complicated, frustrated needs?

Had he underestimated his friend all these years? He wasn't sure. All he knew in this moment was that Bishop's voice seemed to come from some other place. A place not tied to earth or the ordinary but from somewhere celestial, otherworldly.

That night my love strode down the banks by waters opal black

And told me of our hearts and how we might ne'er get them back

The song came to an end and Monty reached for his handkerchief. He was often moved by performances but not to this extent. The tears seemed to flow down his face, and he dabbed them away. He glanced around, slightly embarrassed, but noticed, of his neighbors, he was not the only one to have such a reaction. They seemed at first stunned, before realization struck and they began to applaud.

Monty leaned over to Pearl, "I've not heard that song before. Do you know it?"

"It is an original composition," said Pearl. "Written by your friend."

"No," said Monty. "Bishop wrote that? Unbelievable."

He looked up at his friend who was smiling, and caught his gaze. Monty lifted his hands to clap harder and Bishop.

"We will take a break for now," announced Jade.

They stood and the crowd sprang back into conversational life. Bishop gave Monty a hand signal that he would be just a moment.

Monty nodded and sipped his wine. Pearl and Trevor were engaged in some discussion about the architecture of the room and Monty was content to let them talk. He leaned back in his chair and let his mind wander to the breadth of emotion the last song had inspired in him.

As he sat there, he felt the strongest urge to look behind him. It was the feeling that one has when they feel they are being stared at or watched. Monty tried to ignore it but it became overwhelming, almost as if a force was pushing against his shoulders.

He twisted in his seat, his gaze darting about, and although there were many people behind him, some seated at the tables nearby in clear view, others farther back against the wall, almost mere shadows, he couldn't find anyone with whom to connect his gaze.

He turned back to the table but couldn't shake the feeling that he was being watched.

"I say, isn't that that German fellow?" asked Trevor, interrupting his thoughts. "I thought Bishop had gone off him."

Monty saw Bishop leaned over a table. He was talking to Friedrich, that disquieting man he referred to as "Uncle Freddy."

"Yes," said Monty. "I rather thought he had too."

Monty had assumed that Friedrich was one of Bishop's many lovers when they'd first began their acquaintance. Though he didn't usually take to referring to anyone as Uncle, he did often invent nicknames for his paramours. And although Friedrich's age was somewhat indeterminate, Monty did gauge him to be a bit older and thought it made sense for that reason. Still, after all these months since he'd met Friedrich, he continued to find him off-putting. He realized that Friedrich was serving as Bishop's patron by this point and providing him access to music training he might otherwise not have been able to secure. So when he expressed his wariness to Bishop and Bishop exploded in anger, he knew better than to press his concern. Besides, Bishop had scolded him, he had Trevor, why shouldn't Bishop also be allowed a friend. Monty wondered how much was expected of Bishop in return for this patronage, but he kept those thoughts to himself.

The sense of uneasiness returned now as he studied Friedrich from a distance. Despite his very German name, the man had no discernible accent, and had shared scarce little about himself on the few occasions Monty had spoken with him. He was greying only slightly at the temples, and though his face was unlined and his skin youthful, there was something about him that seemed exceedingly mature, almost ancient, in fact. He wore modern fashions but wore them in a way that they felt like something from another time, his jewelry and embellishments were unique and not at all keeping with any current mode.

The patronage had seemed to pay off in the beginning. Bishop was thrilled with his training and his voice blossomed and blossomed by the month, as he discovered new depths and techniques he had never had access to before. But then his attitude took a turn and he no longer wanted to talk about Friedrich and got snippy when he was mentioned—until finally people stopped bringing him up.

So Monty found it quite odd to see him here, yet again a presence in Bishop's life.

"Excuse me a moment," said Pearl as she rose to speak with Jade who had emerged from backstage.

"Yes, of course," said Trevor.

Monty kept an eye on Bishop as he disengaged himself from Uncle Freddy and was making his way to their table.

Bishop appeared upset, his expression somewhere between worry and anger. But when he saw Monty watching him, he smiled and the consternation dissipated.

"Well, chaps," Bishop said, flopping into the chair just vacated by Pearl, "What did you think?"

Trevor and Monty showered him with praise, and Monty was especially grateful for Trevor's words. He knew that musical outings such as this were not his favorite entertainment but even he too appeared to have been impressed, and Bishop jokingly encouraged more compliments.

Monty tapped his finger on the back of his friend's hand and looked at him with concern.

"Wasn't that your Friedrich, you were talking to just now?"

Bishop winced, and dropped his gaze. "Yes, it was."

"I thought you had cut him," said Monty. "Some months ago, in fact. Things seemed to have gotten quite complicated between you two and you even disappeared for a few weeks. I was quite worried about you, friend, and a moment I wouldn't like to revisit."

"Yes," said Bishop, nodding and picking at the tablecloth. "I remember you were quite upset."

"So why are you associating with him again? He doesn't seem particularly your type. I hope he isn't causing trouble."

Bishop frowned and cleared his throat. He ran his thumb across his lips and then laughed.

"Oh, Monty, you do worry so. I often say I needn't have a mother for as much as you henpeck me," he said with a wink.

"Yes, indeed," agreed Trevor. "I often encourage him to simply live in the moment, but his head seems lost in the future."

Monty didn't like being ganged up on. "Now, see here."

Trevor smiled and rose. "I can see when a chastisement is brewing. I shall minimize my damage by fetching champagne. That always does the trick."

Bishop laughed as Trevor made his way to the bar.

"It's all right, friend," Bishop said to Monty. "I understand your worry, and I appreciate it. Truly I do. But it's pointless. Old Uncle Freddy is nothing to worry about. He poses no danger."

"I didn't mean to suggest danger..." said Monty, startled.

"No, I know. But nothing to worry about at all," reiterated Bishop. "I have Friedrich quite under control, you don't have to think on it. He has his gruff ways, but he has my interests at heart. In fact, he arranged this entire evening."

"Did he?"

"Yes, he financed and organized it and even spread the word about the city. He wanted a showcase of sorts."

"A showcase?"

"You know he has been my patron for quite some time."

"Of course. But you make it sound like he was presenting you to highest bidder."

"Don't be so dramatic, Monty. He only wanted to show off my accomplishments, I suppose. All the work I've put in since I met him. He rather thinks I have a marvelous voice."

"You do, Bishop. Indeed you do. I was even moved to tears."

"Oh, Monty, you're moved to tears at Gilbert and Sullivan."

"Don't make fun," Monty insisted. "Truly. I was moved. In a way I never have been before. Your voice was something otherworldly, if I may use that word. And Pearl says you composed that rather astonishing piece at the end yourself?"

Bishop smiled. "The muses have been much surrounding me of late I suppose. It almost wrote itself."

"It was breathtaking," said Monty. "I am beyond impressed. I never knew you had such depths of talent."

"I suppose I will take that as a compliment," teased Bishop.

"As it was meant. And those lyrics, where did you come up with that sentiment?"

"Is it really so remarkable as that?"

"Unexpected more like."

Bishop smiled. "I suppose I was thinking of someone particular, from the past, but also I suppose—"

His smile fell and he stopped speaking, staring over Monty's shoulder.

Monty turned and half expected to see Uncle Freddy but instead he saw Trevor talking to a gen-

tleman he didn't recognize at first. He wondered
what could have affected Bishop so until he realized
who Trevor was talking to. It was Reginald Canestre,
son of Viscount Heamton with whom they'd gone
to school. And who Bishop had fallen in love with,
utterly and completely, though he had never owned
up to it.

Trevor glanced at them nervously as he approached the table. No doubt worried about making
introductions in such an establishment where he
ought not to be, Monty thought. Trevor was always
preoccupied with presenting an acceptable face to
everyone. Any whiff of the suggestion of a scandal turned him ashen. Sometimes Monty wondered
how he managed to accept the more Bohemian set
with which Monty and Bishop surrounded themselves. He decided to assuage some of the encroach-
ing anxiety in Trevor's expression.

"Leggy, is that you?" Monty called out.

Reginald turned to him. "Montgomery Singer? I
should have known if Bishop was about you would
be nearby. By god, Monty, how are you?"

Monty stood to shake his hand.

"Quite good, old bean. I didn't know you knew
Lord Mawnton."

"Yes, Trevor and I have known each other since I
was in short pants. His father and mine have always
been great friends."

Trevor nodded, visibly relieved.

"Yes," he said. "Reggie's older brother and I used
to shoot together quite a bit. But I wasn't aware you
knew Mister Singer and Lord Brookesbay."

"Yes," said Monty. "We were at school together. Leggy and Bishop and I were quite the trio."

"We might still be if given half the chance," piped up Bishop from the table, seemingly recovered from his earlier moment of mute shock.

Leggy's smile broadened and he moved to the table.

"Did you come to see me sing, darling?" asked Bishop, his social bravado restored.

"Of course. I've only arrived in Paris three days ago, but I heard you would be performing. You don't think I would miss such an opportunity."

Bishop smiled a crooked smile. "I should hope not, no."

Melancholy tugged at Monty's chest, seeing Bishop and Leggy reunited. It was always such sentiment when Leggy returned. He was always drifting in and out of Bishop's life, though his last drift in had been some time ago. Neither could release the other, it was clear to Monty and he knew, in fact in more than one overly drunken occasion at some party or club back home had been told by Leggy, always on the verge of tears, that he would drop any other attachments and come to Bishop's side if he would only ask. But Bishop was hesitant, forever wary of letting himself get too attached to one man.

"There is no future for two chaps together in this world," he had once told Monty.

"That's not true," Monty had argued. "There are many who find a way."

"Those that do don't have the familial obligations and duty that I have, Monty. It's terrible enough that my own heart must be broken by such responsibility, I cannot ask another to willingly sacrifice his own as well."

"Ah, the champagne," said Trevor.

Monty turned and saw one of the bedeviled wait-staff, dressed in some sort of Hell-inspired costume, with a tray of champagne and glasses. He let the server pass and then joined his friends at the table.

"No, I mean every word," said Leggy. "I knew you had a voice—I fondly remember us singing together on many an occasion. But I never knew it to be as marvelous as that."

"Perhaps you only chose to hear it as such, dear Leggy."

"Here," said Trevor, passing around the filled flutes. "What's with all this Leggy business?"

"At the beginning of second term," Leggy explained, "I sprained my ankle something awful. So for weeks, I was hobbling and limping around, and Bishop here took to calling me Reggy Leggy. All the other boys took it up and it stuck."

"I supposed that was rather awful of me," said Bishop. "How did you ever cope with me?"

"Not awful at all," Leggy objected. "It is a school honor to receive a brand new name. And I rather thought of it as my pet name, given me by you. Which, of course, made it all the more special."

Bishop had the damnable nerve to blush.

Trevor looked shocked. To see such doe-eyed affection between two fellows displayed in public, in the midst of a crowd of people and not hidden away in privacy, likely shook him to his core. It almost made Monty chuckle.

"So you liked the songs then this evening?" Bishop asked, almost shyly.

"How could one not?" exclaimed Leggy. "Most especially that last one. Something about it seemed to speak directly to me, as if it were formed from very own soul."

"Bishop wrote that one, you know," offered Monty.

"Did you? But that's extraordinary," said Leggy.

"Not so much as that," argued Bishop.

As they continued to flirt, Monty picked up his glass of champagne for a sip. In doing so, he glanced towards the booth where Friedrich was sitting and found the man glowering in their direction, watching Bishop and Leggy with the utmost intensity. His eyes were like those of a python rearing back to strike. It was not just mere jealousy Monty saw in the expression but something far more sinister.

"Won't you come to my apartments tonight?" Trevor asked, bringing his attention back. "Come stay the night with me."

Monty smiled. "Have you had that much champagne?"

"What do you mean?"

"You have never had me back to your rooms. In fact, you insist that we stay overnight only at mine. I know you worry we might be seen."

Trevor grabbed Monty's hand and lifted it to his lips, kissing it.

"Forget all that," said Trevor. "And, no, I am not drunk. I know what I want and tonight I don't give a damn what anybody thinks. Maybe it's the music, maybe it's this bizarre little cavern of sin, but I am feeling untethered. Won't you give me some of your time, Monty?"

Monty pulled Trevor's hand to his lips and kissed it in kind.

"As much time as you would like, dear sir."

They enjoyed their glasses and their two spheres of conversation until Bishop sat forward.

"It will soon be time for our second set," he said.

"Must you go?" asked Leggy.

"I must, but that does not mean you must stay."

"No?"

"Come with me, now. I'll show you the next songs. You can sing harmony with Jade, she won't mind at all."

"Oh, but, Bishop, are you sure? I shouldn't want to intrude."

"In no way would you," Bishop replied, standing. He grabbed Leggy's hand and pulled him up from his chair. "Come."

"I've never seen your friend like that," said Trevor with a chuckle. "He has certainly brightened up almost instantly. Reginald seems a tonic for him."

"Some people are like that. They give you light even when you are covered in shadow."

"Indeed. I quite know exactly how he feels," Said Trevor, his voice full of longing.

Trevor leaned forward then and kissed him. Monty was surprised—Trevor had never kissed him outside of closed doors – but quickly returned the kiss with as much passion as it was given.

"Now," said Trevor. "What shall we do tomorrow then?"

Monty listened as he listed all the things he would like him and Monty to do. After a moment, Monty became distracted, as a queer feeling overtook him.

Again he felt as if he were being watched somehow. He looked over at where Uncle Freddy was seated, but the man was not facing him, instead conversing with the pianist—in a very pointed way, it appeared. No, the feeling was coming from behind, Monty was sure of it. He turned in his seat again and but no one nearby was noticing him. He cast his eyes to the balcony area above.

His eyes came to stop on the silhouette of what appeared to be a very tall man with broad shoulders. In the ridiculous atmosphere of the club, Monty could not make out any more details from his vantage point. But he somehow felt sure that this man was staring at him, though he hadn't the foggiest notion as to why. He squinted against the red glow of the torches and tried to make out anything more but to no avail. He felt compelled to stand and thought he ought to head upstairs to see just exactly who this person was.

"Good lord, Monty, are you even listening to me?"

Trevor's voice snapped him back. He felt as if he had awoken from a trance. He sat down suddenly, shaking his head.

"I apologize, Trevor. I'm not sure what came over me."

"Are you quite all right? What were you staring at?"

"I don't know," said Monty. "I suppose I saw somebody I thought I knew. Or something like that."

"I think that's enough champagne for the evening," said Trevor in a soothing tone.

"Yes, perhaps it ought to be."

Pearl returned to the table.

"Oh, *superbe*! Champagne. May I?"

"Yes, of course," said Trevor. "Do help yourself."

"Have you ever seen such a crowd of people?" she asked, after a long refreshing sip. "Anybody and everybody with good taste is here this evening."

"Yes. Well, it does seem rather crowded," said Trevor.

The pianist ran his fingers lightly across a sequence of keys.

"Here we are," said Pearl. "More delicious music."

As Bishop and Jade, now with Leggy in tow, returned to the stage Monty looked towards "Uncle Freddy" again. Friedrich was watching the trio on stage quite intently. His face wore an inscrutable expression but one that boded nothing good, Monty was sure. Friedrich lifted his pipe to his mouth and inhaled, the embers in the bowl of the instrument glowing hotter and redder than the lights which fell on him. Monty felt an involuntary shiver run over him, and turned away, directing his attention to the stage.

Just as the song began, and all were concentrating on the stage, Monty stole a glance over his shoulder. He turned his attention back to the balcony, but the man he thought he had seen before was gone.

His eyes danced around the room but no shadow or silhouette seemed to match the form he had observed watching.

Perhaps Trevor was right; perhaps he was over-come with drink.

Could he have imagined it?

He had never been accused of not having a more than healthy imagination. Monty thought back to his sketchbook and the unknown man who always sprang from his pencil. Maybe he was a bit of a fantasist. Still, the feeling was so strong, he didn't see how it couldn't be real.

Chapter Seven

London, 1910

M onty sat in the barrel-style armchair that he had dragged across the room. One foot propped on the windowsill, he pushed back, balancing the chair on its hind legs. He looked out at the city below, just falling into evening. The street lamps had been lit and all over lamps twinkled in windows, a second set of stars emerging against the night sky.

With frustration, he snatched the sketchbook which he had draped across his knee and flipped through the most recent pages. Unable to rest or relax since they'd arrived at the townhouse, he'd finally taken up his sketchbook and tried to distract his mind. But try as he might, all his hand seemed to want to draw were more and more images of that damned gorgeous selkie-man who was in the room beside him.

No longer were the drawings incomplete— faceless and unfinished. Now they came fully formed, all of Rodin's exquisite features appearing from the dark lead of his pencil tip. Various expressions and moods expressed, the curve of his lips in a frown, the rise of his brows in surprise, even the sparkle of his lovely golden brown eyes, all there on the pages. Monty cursed the weakness of his mind, and turned to a clean page, pressing its center hard against the spine of the notebook as if to create a wall between the blankness and the images of Rodin before.

He would compose a list, he decided. All the questions he needed answered from Weaver on how exactly this magical creature had appeared and why, very much why, he seemed to be created from Monty's dreams. But as he studied at the creamy expanse before him, no words came to his mind, only eyes and lips, and supple golden skin.

A rapping at the door startled him. He hoped Bishop wasn't ready to begin the night's hunt just yet. Monty wanted a little more time to clear his head. And he could use just some more separation from Rodin, his body still raw and unsettled from the queer feelings he'd had from that touch earlier. The rapping continued and he stood, tossing his sketchbook onto the nearby table.

"Sir," a shaky voice called from the other side of the door. "Sir, are you there?"

Now Monty was confused. Why would Bishop have sent a servant after him? He had insisted that he didn't need valeting.

"I'm sorry to disturb, sir, but if you are there, please..."

Monty hastily opened the door. "Yes?"

The abashed young man stepped back. "Sorry to disturb you, sir. It's only that—well, he was asking for you. It seemed urgent, sir."

"Lord Brookesbay?"

"No, sir. The other one, the darker one."

The young man had a very disturbed look on his face and Monty thought back to earlier in the day at the lake when Rodin first transformed in the car. Monty thanked him and rushed next door. As he turned the knob, he heard some very odd noises coming from within. He moved quickly, anxious and, frankly, a little frightened at what he might find inside.

Rodin was at the foot of the bed, doubled over, clutching onto the bedclothes with one hand and gripping his midsection with the other. As Monty got closer, Rodin held out his arm, his fingers shaking, as if reaching for help.

"Monty," he cried out breathlessly. And then he let out a small howl of pain and fell to his knees.

The misery in the man was evident and Monty forgot all anxiety as he rushed to him, determined to somehow help.

"What is it? What can I do?"

Rodin had stripped off all of his clothing save his trousers, and as Monty put his hands around his neck, trying to support him, his skin was wet with perspiration and seemed to be flashing hot and cold under his very touch. The muscles of Rodin's back convulsed weirdly, as if they were rolling like a wave, and Monty heard a disturbing cracking noise.

"Monty," Rodin gasped.

"Yes, yes, I'm here. Are you ill? What do I need to do?"

"W-w-wa—" But the sound broke off before he could complete what he was saying and turned into a loud bark. It was the same barking sound they had heard this morning at the lake. Rodin moaned in seeming pain and barked again.

"W-w-w-water," he finally managed to say.

"Yes, yes, of course!" cried Monty. He must return to the water it seemed. But how in the hell would he get him to a lake or even the river from here? It seemed impossible.

Rodin thrashed about, his body convulsing, and he let out a series of barks.

Monty dashed for the door and flung it open. Down at the end of the hall was the same footman from before, he seemed to be hovering at the top of the stairs.

"You there! What's your name?"

The young man jumped, and slowly backed into the hallway.

"Black, sir. Henry Black."

"Do you have a bath in the house, Henry? With a tub?"

"Yes, sir, we have room just at the end of this wing. Roll top bateau," he added proudly. "From Paris that is."

"Yes, lovely. Could you please make sure it is filled immediately? We have urgent need."

"For the bath, sir?"

"Yes, please."

He looked over his shoulder at Rodin writhing on the floor, moaning. There was no way he could carry him alone, in this state, and he couldn't possibly involve the footman any more than he was already.

"And Lord Brookesbay, where is he, do we know?"

"Just downstairs, with the guests."

"Good man," said Monty, pulling the door closed. "Now, please, make haste on that tub!"

Henry scrambled off down the hallway and Monty dashed for the stairs.

Downstairs, as he hurried towards the main drawing room from which the noise of the assembled party emanated, he realized he was only wearing his shirt, trousers, and socks. He couldn't worry about that now. Something was happening upstairs and the need to get Rodin to water appeared more than urgent enough to discount scandal. Damn, why the devil had they brought that creature to the city? It was his own stupid suggestion at that. What a fool he had been—nervous and disturbed by his own worries of some sort of black magic. Too blinded by his own fraught emotions to think of the logic of removing the man too far from his habitat.

Monty reached the drawing room and peered in, through the crowd, larger than he had expected, looking for his friend. He saw Bishop near a window speaking with two men, and tried to call out.

"Bishop!" he said in a loud stage whisper. "Bishop!"

His friend turned his head and, seeing Monty, waved at him to come over, returning to his conversation. Monty ground his teeth and slipped his way into the milling people.

"My dear Monty," he heard Aunt Charlotte say, "I am rather Bohemian, I admit it, but I do prefer that my guests at least arrive in shoes."

"My apologies, Lady Denglarry, but there's a bit of a situation with our friend and I need Bishop's assistance."

"Anything I can help with? I can send someone up now. We've far too many footmen milling about the place, really."

"Oh, no, thank you. It's only a spot of illness, I'm sure, that can suddenly overtake our friend. Bishop is familiar with how to help."

Aunt Charlotte nodded wisely. "Yes, I see. Bishop!" she called out, turning towards her nephew. "Come here now, please!"

Seeming flustered, Bishop appeared in seconds.

"Yes, yes, what's all this then? I was just talking to the most marvelous pair, you'll never guess who."

"Come with me," said Monty. "Now, please."

"Whatever is the matter, Monty, that can't wait? And why are you in such *déshabillé*? You haven't even changed yet."

"It's your friend, the Portuguese one," offered Aunt Charlotte. "Apparently, he needs you."

"Yes, he's having one of his moments," said Monty tightly. Bishop looked blank. "Like this morning? By the lake?"

Light dawned. "Oh, I say. Yes, let's go then. Won't be a moment, Aunt."

The two men rushed up to Rodin's room, Monty almost dragging Bishop up the stairs, and found him in the same terrible state on the floor as Monty had left him.

"Great God in heaven" exclaimed Bishop. "Is he turning back?"

"It would seem that way," said Monty, rushing to kneel by the moaning man.

Monty had to close his eyes and turn his head away once he saw Rodin. His face had begun to change and was somewhere between that of a man and that of a round-faced seal, the bones and features shifting like the rolling and cresting of waves. Only the eyes seemed to have remained the same, and they looked filled with pain. His torso had puffed out into a great belly, and fur had come in all over him. His arms jerked like the flippers of a dolphin might, the fingers on his hands fused together and changing. The trousers had been ripped off as the legs had come together and seemed also to be morphing by the minute. Monty was surprised he had not changed back faster, but the progress seemed to be blessedly slower than earlier in the day. Rodin lay gasping on the floor, his breathing rough and ragged, like a fish pulled from the sea, and his barks more like wheezing coughs.

"We must get him to the bath."

Bishop stuck his head into the hallway. Coming in his direction he saw Henry.

"You there!" he called out and the young man jumped.

"Yes, sir. I've filled the bath as your friend asked, all ready to go. I wasn't sure if there was enough warm water but I let it run to the top just in case, so it might be a bit cool, sir. Sorry, sir."

"Not at all, well done—what's your name?"

"Black, sir. Henry Black."

"Well done, Henry. Now, I need you to go to Mister Davies and have him give you the biggest and best towels that we have in the linen closet. As many as he can spare. Tell him I insist and that he shouldn't argue."

"Yes, sir."

"And quick, quick, please, Henry. Run if you must."

"Yes, sir," Henry answered and scampered off.

"Now, all is clear," said Bishop, over his shoulder.

"Help me with him," commanded Monty. "You take his legs and I'll take him up top."

Bishop did as bade and soon they were whisking Rodin down the hallway, though not as quickly as they might have being weighed down by his enormous girth. Monty stole a look at Rodin's face as they moved and saw those pained eyes staring at him.

"It's all just fine now," he assured Rodin and the selkie answered with a weak little bark.

"Oh blast," Bishop cursed as they reached the door. "The bloody boy's closed it."

He shifted Rodin's weight to his hip, turned the knob and then kicked it open. Without waiting they rushed to the tub, and dropped the selkie in it. Water splashed up on all sides, soaking their trousers and Bishop's shoes. Monty was unsure whether to submerge Rodin's head in the water or not, but as soon as he hit the surface Rodin submerged him-self. There was a moving and thrashing underneath which only brought up more water and Bishop jumped back.

Monty stood, transfixed, as the water splashed and Rodin flapped about underneath. After a moment, his head emerged just at the lip of the tub, now fully in his selkie form and he barked a bright, happy bark. Monty found himself laughing in relief and felt the urge to pet the creature's head. Rodin pushed back from the side of the tub, smacking his foreflippers together, and gave a little yelp before letting himself fall back into the lukewarm water, again sending a little wave onto the floor.

To one side of the bathing room there was a wood-en bench against the wall and Bishop was already seated, removing his shoes. Monty sat down beside him and began to peel off his own sodden socks.

"It's lucky I brought that enormous case after all," Bishop said dryly.

"Not exactly the eventualities you were expect-ing?"

"Not exactly, no. But I'll need to change again before we go out."

"If we go out, you mean," said Monty.

"But why wouldn't we? You don't mean he won't change back at all?"

"I haven't the foggiest, dear Bishop. I am not well studied on the habits of mythical creatures, after all."

"Now see here," said Bishop, his tone irascible, "Are we meant to sit here all evening babysitting him? And how am I to explain a great, noisome seal in the tub come morning?"

From the tub, Rodin, who had poked his head above the water let out a chiding bark.

"We've heard quite enough from you this evening, thank you!" Bishop called back. "I don't care if you can bark in five languages, keep it to yourself."

Rodin let out a noise which sounded something like a scoff before he reclined back into the water.

Monty sighed. "I'm sure your aunt would be understanding. She is extraordinarily open-minded, after all."

"There is open-minded, Monty, and then there is absurd. Besides, this is not my aunt's home and I don't suppose my parents would look too kindly upon an aquatic zoo in their London townhouse, however disused."

"Well, if needs must, we'll bundle him back into your great Baker and whisk him back to Manchester Lake."

"What will the servants say when we carry him out of the house?"

"You're of the upper classes, Bishop, the servants expect you to do absurd, unexplainable things."

Bishop considered this.

"Yes, I see your point."

There was a knock at the door.

"That will be the linens, I imagine," said Bishop as he got up to answer it.

Henry had indeed returned with a stack of the best towels on offer in the house. He had five in his arms and they came up to just his chin.

"Good man, thank you very much," said Bishop, taking them from him. "You might have Davies send up some more though. I did not exaggerate when I said all he could spare."

Henry took a quick glance down at Bishop's naked feet.

"Yes, sir."

"And while you're at it, tell him to prepare one or two mops and buckets as well. There may be need of some cleanup."

"Now, sir?"

"Hopefully soon, but I'll send word."

Just then there was a bright series of barks from the tub. Henry's eyes went wide.

"Is everything all right, sir?" asked the young man as he tried to peer into the room.

Bishop moved his body to block the view. "Quite all right, thank you, Henry. If you could fetch some more towels, as I said. And you might just leave them here outside the door for us to retrieve as needed."

"Yes, sir. But is there anything I can help with—"

"Just the towels. Thank you, Henry."

Bishop closed the door and turned to peer at the selkie with a scolding look.

"You really are too much to be believed."

"Oh, do sit down, Bishop. Aren't you the one who admonished me about being adventurous? Here we are then."

"Did I say that? How stupid of me. Remind me of this moment next time I say anything so thought-less."

Monty got up and took the towels from Bishop, spreading a couple of them on the floor to absorb the small pond that had formed.

"Sit," he said as he did this, "and tell me about this marvelous pair you were talking with."

Bishop flopped onto the bench and carefully laid his soaked stockings on the end to dry.

"It was Thomas Cullen, from school, you remember him? Lord Fielding?"

Monty straightened the towels on the floor and headed for the bench himself.

"Yes, of course, I remember. How could I not? He was the best-looking man at school."

Rodin gave a short little bark from the tub.

"I beg your pardon?" said Bishop.

Monty leaned against the wall, suddenly exhausted.

"Yes, yes. The best-looking man at school apart from you. Now tell me about Thomas and his fascinating companion."

"The chap goes by the name of Baldwin and he's a writer. You've probably read him; he writes those Lady Detective stories."

"The Beatrice Cavendish mysteries? Oh, yes, I adore those. But I thought a woman wrote them."

"*Nom de plume*, darling. Apparently he resides in Thomas's home in the city—quite the infamous household—and, it turns out, they have a printing press in the basement of the place."

"Do they print the Lady Detective mysteries themselves?"

"No, those are handled by a regular publisher. But here's the interesting part: their press is reserved for rather more, shall we say, niche works. As it turns out this Baldwin chap is in fact the author of *Gifts for the Sheikh* as well."

"No! Really? That one is all the talk. Has been for months. Quite scandalous."

"I'm well aware; I've read it twice myself. He says he is working on another new story, just for the gentleman, of course. Thomas swore me to secrecy, so you must not say a word, but he knows I am the height of discretion."

"Apart from telling me all?"

Bishop sniffed. "That's different. Everyone knows you're my best friend. They can't possibly expect that I'd keep anything from you."

Monty folded one of the dry towels and placed it behind his head against the wall.

"Imagine," Monty said. "Being able to make one's living from doing something like that. To get money from art, wouldn't it be amazing to live like that?"

"Is your father still at you to join the family business?"

"Not like he used to be. My sister is very keen to learn the business, and although he isn't quite sure of women working, I think he appreciates her interest. Besides, although he used to accuse me of being a wastrel, I think he rather likes my aimlessness now. He thinks it makes me like the sons of his aristocratic friends."

"Hear now, that's rather rude, isn't it. Insinuating that we're all lazy."

"Possibly rude," admitted Monty. He looked at Bishop with a cheeky smile. "But also possibly quite truthful."

"Maybe you ought not to worry so much about what your father or anybody else thinks and do what you want," Bishop countered. "Embrace the magic, Monty. Be who you are."

"You're a fine one to talk. You had one of the best voices around and were even starting to compose before we went to France. Then suddenly you stopped with no explanation whatsoever."

Bishop exhaled deeply. "I could use a cigarette."

"Further to the point," continued Monty, "I come back from America and find you ensconced in the country, building yourself into quite the respectable gentleman."

"I'm hardly respectable in anyone's eyes but yours, Monty. And I did not abandon music at all—I was... well, I had to give it up. That's all. And besides, our situations are not the same."

Monty pursed his lips. "You're a second son, Bishop, you don't bear that much of the family burden."

"That's not at all what I mean. And I believe my father might disagree with you on that score. What I mean is, unlike me, you are truly talented, a real artist. If only you would believe it."

"Hogwash. You're a brilliant musician."

"You're avoiding my point. But my music is neither here nor there anymore. It's not an option for me. But it could be something real for you. You still have the ability to bring your dreams to life. The only thing holding you back from making it reality is you."

Monty sat forward. He gazed at Rodin splashing around in the tub, struck by the weight of Bishop's accusation.

"I thought I might have a chance. Back in France." Monty twisted the towel in his hands. "When Mister Woo managed to sell some of my art to those Americans. That felt like something."

"Is that how you came up with the ridiculous name for our aquatic companion?"

"Yes, I suppose so," Monty conceded. "Seeing him there in your bedroom earlier, it struck something in me. I couldn't fathom such magic just appearing out of the blue. It's suspect. But I realized I hadn't been shaken up since those days in Paris, when everything felt so raw and new. I think the bizarre nature of it all reawakened a small fire within me."

Bishop gave him a sly look. "Yes, obviously. Quite the fire I should say."

Monty shook his head. "No, I don't mean that. Well, not only that. I can't have my artistic sensibility awakened by my libido, can I? Isn't that entirely vulgar?"

"Passion is passion, darling. It's all interconnected. How many great creatives in history have simply wanted to fuck their muse? The fire is fed how the fire is fed."

"But it isn't only fire I feel."

"Of course not. And that's why you are an artist, no matter how much you protest."

Monty turned to his friend.

"You know, for someone who plays dim, you have quite profound depths."

"Don't let's tell anyone, please," said Bishop. "The last person anyone wants to invite to their dinner party is someone 'profound.'"

There was a knock at the door.

"I told that boy just to leave the towels outside," said Bishop.

"I'll see to it," said Monty.

He answered the door.

"Oh hello, sir," said Henry. "You're in here too then?"

"Yes, Henry. As I am the one who asked you to draw the bath, that shouldn't be entirely shocking, should it? "

"No, sir. Of course not, sir. Just wondering if everything was okay, or if you needed anything?"

"Goodness, I do say," Bishop exclaimed from inside the room.

Monty glanced over his shoulder and his eyes widened a bit.

"Yes, thank you, Henry," Monty said quickly as he grabbed the new supply of towels and shut the door.

Monty turned to find Rodin standing in the bath, water trickling down his body. Monty tried not to gape at his body which seemed somehow fuller and altogether more magnificent than before, if that were possible.

"Just at the right moment," Monty said.

He walked over to the tub, extending his arms and offering the towels. Rodin stepped out and stood in front of Monty. He did not take the towels but rather lifted his arms at his sides and stared at Monty, waiting.

"I think he wants you to do the honors," offered Bishop.

"Yes, I rather got that impression," said Monty. "I am not your servant, Rodin."

"No. You are not," agreed the man. Still he did not move.

"Well, we simply can't let him drip dry," exclaimed Bishop. "We'll be here until dawn. Just do it, Monty."

Monty sighed and dropped the towels to the floor. He grabbed the top one and unfurled it before him. It spread out enormously.

"This is like some great Turkish *hammam* towel."

"Mamma does like her linens," said Bishop

"Where shall I begin?" asked Monty.

Rodin offered no reply except a smile.

As Monty began to rub the cotton towel over Rodin's massive chest, Bishop stood.

"Now, Rodin, tell me," said Bishop, in his best Lord of the Manor tone. "Will this—happening—be occurring regularly? Must we plan to carry a great zinc tub around with us throughout the night?"

"I don't think so," answered Rodin. "Usually I can control the change, but sometimes, if I am emotional, I lose command over my body. Sometimes my body makes its own demands."

Rodin smiled at Monty and dropped his eyes down. Monty's gaze follow and suddenly the towel got hung up. Monty blushed and snatched it free.

"You certainly seemed to have gained quite a command over the English language during your immersion," said Bishop, thankfully not acknowledging what he had just seen.

Rodin answered Bishop but his eyes found Monty's. "I am a quick study. Would you mind doing my back as well?"

Monty inhaled deeply and nodded, as Rodin turned, presenting his glistening backside.

"Before you two turn all the remaining water into steam, I shall head to my room to change," said Bishop. "If you make demands enough of your body to keep it in human form, Rodin, perhaps the two of you can join me shortly ready to proceed with our plans for the evening? I certainly didn't come to London to mop floors."

"Yes, yes, Bishop, we understand," answered Monty.

"Shan't be a tick, yes?" Rodin offered.

Bishop opened the door to find the young footman standing there still.

"Henry, what a surprise," Bishop said flatly.

Henry was nervously stepping from one foot to the other. He looked bashful.

"Only to let you know, sir, that your gentleman friend's suit is ready and has been left in his room."

"Splendid."

Henry cleared his throat. "Is there anything else you might need, sir?"

Bishop narrowed his eyes, and smiled slyly.

"I can't think of anything, Henry. Is there some need you might anticipate us having which you could fulfill?"

Henry's neck flushed red, and he dropped his eyes, a smile at his lips. "No, sir, nothing I can think of, I reckon."

"Perhaps later, when we've returned from our evening plans, there may be needs which arise. But I am sure we do appreciate your attentiveness at any rate."

"Yes, sir," answered Henry, tugging at the front of his waistcoat. "Thank you, sir."

He turned then and scuttled down the hallway, casting one last glance back at Bishop before disappearing behind the green baize door.

"You really are incorrigible," said Monty.

Bishop found both men behind him. He looked up at the towering Rodin, who was wrapped in the towel.

"You haven't gotten taller too, have you?"

"I do not think so," said Rodin.

"I suggest you don't. We can't get you to the tailor for at least another twelve hours, and I do not intend to carry a needle and thread on my person for any of your... future eruptions."

Chapter Eight

The front drawing room was now even more crowded than when Monty had come down earlier seeking Bishop. The smaller blue drawing room across the foyer had quickly filled with people as well, being turned into an ad hoc casino of sorts, it appeared. Monty saw small tables and chairs had been set up all around the room as partygoers engaged in card games. Someone had discovered a phonograph in the main drawing room and music filled the entire lower floor from it. Monty stood to the side, nursing a cocktail, and watching the crowd.

He had changed into his evening attire, all ready for their proposed trip to the Brunswick, but a new set of doubts had beset him. The conversation by the tub with Bishop had awakened a set of emotions in him. He realized he had been content these last few years to move with the currents of life, to float placidly along the surface. But this mad day had broken something loose within him. Now things were not predictable—not only just the course of a normal day, but the normal order of the world. A transforming creature as beautiful as a siren, and possibly as dangerous, had appeared as if Monty had carved him from marble by means of his own two hands. And Bishop's cagey talk of things occult and his shady past with this Weaver character. What parts of life had he not noticed; how numb had he kept himself? This rawness, this energy, this restlessness, these are the things he thought he had tamped down within himself.

He had let himself be carried by this typhoon of emotions before, and it had nearly drowned him. He couldn't let that happen again. Yet he felt powerless to resist its undertow.

"I come bearing refreshed refreshments," declared Bishop, appearing by Monty's side, a drink in each hand. "And look who I found contemplating mortality by the drinks cart. Our dear Pearson."

Pearson was a close friend and old friend of both Monty and Bishop, and though they would both claim otherwise, he and Bishop shared a very close bond. Neither of them particularly cared for anyone to know this so they covered it with a perpetual shower of insults.

"I was simply in hiding," said Pearson. "I've been trying to avoid that rather large American friend of your aunt all evening. He has had his sights locked on me since I arrived, like some tiger hunt straight out of Kipling."

"I'm sure that's a literary reference that Monty will understand," said Bishop. "I've never had the time to read Kipling myself."

"Pearson, good to see you." Monty greeted him with a nod. "Where is your Mister Laurence this evening?"

"Yes, so rarely are you devoid of his company," added Bishop, his tone wry, "that I was shocked to find you ambulatory without him holding up one side of you."

Pearson pointedly ignored this jape and answered Monty.

"Jonas is tromping through the countryside on a tour of homes in need of horticultural assistance. But I'm afraid he is no longer my Mister Laurence, at any rate."

"No," replied Monty with genuine concern. "Has something happened?"

"Distinctly nothing has happened, I think is the better way to put it. We've been growing apart for some time, as you might have noticed." He removed one of the drinks from Bishop's hand and gulped it down. "Thank you. Now, anyway, let's not talk of all that. Water under the bridge, you know."

"Or perhaps mist over the wisteria?" supplied Bishop.

"Bishop tells me you're heading for the Brunswick. I do hope to tag along, if it's not a burden."

"Of course not," said Monty. "We're taking a new friend anyhow."

"Where is our new friend by the way?" asked Bishop.

"He's still dressing."

"Himself?" asked Bishop with a raised brow.

"No, I caught that Henry on my way down and asked him to check in on Rodin, see if he might need some help in the valeting style."

"Oh, check her, darling, she's probably trying to take his clothes off not put them on," said Bishop.

"Rodin," said Pearson. "He's this French friend Bishop mentioned to me?"

"Yes," said Monty. "We're hoping to introduce him to Weaver."

"The Weaver?" replied Pearson. "You didn't mention that part, Bishop. Whatever do you want him for?"

"We think he might have a few things to share with our new friend. They have similar interests," said Bishop.

"Hmm. Interesting," said Pearson, seemingly unconvinced. "Well, good luck finding him."

"Is he not in town?" asked Monty.

"Oh, he's very much here," said Pearson. "Spending most of his time with his new companion, however. An American woman with a great mane of hair. Which looks hennaed to me, I might add. Wears great frocks. Less like a respectable dress and more like something one might find in a Tunisian harem."

"Rather a specific reference," quipped Bishop.

"And covered in jewels," continued Pearson. "Not at all rude in the usual American way, even if she looks quite odd. But she is pleasant and interesting—quite the most interesting person on the scene in some time."

"Apparently," said Bishop.

"Is she much younger than him?" asked Monty, intrigued.

"Who could possibly not be?" responded Pearson. "Daniel Weaver must be at least a century old."

"What are you gents over here scheming up?" A loud voice boomed behind them.

They all turned in surprise to find Mister Anderson Herald.

"Where's that Adonis of a friend of yours?" Anderson asked Monty.

"He'll be down shortly."

"I certainly hope so. Glad to have all you fellows here; nice to have some young blood in the mix."

"Quite," replied Bishop as he sipped his drink.

"Now," Anderson said, turning to Pearson. "You promised you would join us for a rubber of bridge."

"Did I? The memory fails."

"You did. And Charlotte's getting antsy to play. The others have already paired off and we're one short; we need you to make a complete set. Don't make me throw you over my shoulder and carry you into the room."

"I wouldn't dream of it," said Pearson, snatching what was left of Bishop's drink from his hand.

"Splendid," said Anderson. He elbowed Bishop and winked. "Your aunt sure does like to gamble, doesn't she?"

"In all of areas of her life," Bishop replied dryly.

"Poor Pearson," said Monty as he was escorted by Anderson across the foyer.

"He's wrangled free of worse clutches in his day."

The disc on the phonograph came to a sudden halt and there was a cry for some music as a willowy young man dashed to the piano situated near Monty and Bishop.

"Time for some real music," the pianist called out. "Do we have anyone who might sing for me?"

"Ah, look," said Bishop quickly. "There's old Jodh-purs who we met at that Maximalist propaganda meeting which you dragged me to last summer."

"It was a discussion of Russian poetry, Bishop, and I believe his name is Jasper."

"Yes, yes. The point being I've been hoping to see him, whatever he's called, ever since."

Monty shook his head as Bishop made a beeline for the attractive man from the summer past. He stayed where he was and leaned against the wall, listening to the music. One young lady, dressed in a striking evening gown, columnar and made of rasp-berry-colored silk with an open neckline, trotted up to make a request. She seemed to tiptoe as she made her way over and her mass of loosely piled curls moved as if they might all abandon ship at any moment and cascade down her back.

"It's called the Boston, darling, do you know it?" Monty heard her ask.

"Of course I do," the willowy young man at the piano proclaimed. "You know I've just spent a season in America—New York to be precise. I even bought a gramophone whilst I was there. All of the new records, you know. Some amazing ragtime stuff. I might even bring them to the next party, if you'll be there to listen?"

"I can't think why I shouldn't be," the young woman said demurely. "But if you could just play the little waltz for me, I would be ever so grateful."

The young man seemed delighted to fulfill her request, and as he began to play and the young woman grabbed a nearby girlfriend to whom to show the steps of the dance, Monty surveyed the congregation of people as the music kicked into gear. Some folks were in conversation, some were smoking cigarettes and others substances whose scent Monty did not recognize, and almost all were drinking cocktails, which Aunt Charlotte insisted upon in place of the *"dusty old"* port and brandy. A few even had a hazy expression that suggested a touch too much laudanum or something similar. Monty thought back to Aunt Charlotte's earlier words and agreed that this was not at all the type of party that Lady Brookesbay, Bishop's mother, would have hosted.

He wondered, too, how angry Lady Brookesbay might be now that both he and Bishop had fled. At least it would have left her with two young ladies unattended, who might have to keep one another company, instead of a third odd man. Monty did give a moment of grief for the young ladies. After all, they certainly wouldn't be doing anything as excitingly fashionable as the Boston. And although he was sure neither would have been particularly sad to have missed him, so many young girls in the county held out hope that Bishop might finally secure a wife and would be sorely disappointed to have missed an opportunity to further their acquaintance with the second born of such an illustrious family. He looked over at Bishop, working his charms on Old Jodhpurs and smiled. If only those poor young ladies knew the truth of their chances.

Monty had a sudden sensation of being watched, and he turned in the doorway of the room. He saw Rodin descending the stairs.

Their eyes met.

Mister Anderson's wardrobe had proved much the better fit and Monty could not deny how dashing Rodin appeared—he might have even admitted to absolutely ravishing. Whatever maid had worked the garments deserved celebration for her deft hand. The alterations fit him like a glove. Apparently, Henry had not been able to find a proper evening waistcoat so Rodin was decked out in a royal purple waistcoat and a matching paisley cravat, to cover the neck that not even the bulky American's collar could contain. On anyone else it might have looked gaudy but Rodin wore it like a prince, and it gave him a glamorous allure.

Rodin strode over to Monty and before he could protest, grabbed his hand and brought it to his lips. He kissed the back of Monty's hand as if Monty were a foreign duchess being presented at court. It might have struck anyone observing as slightly ridiculous, but the touch of Rodin's lips against his skin sent a thunderbolt through Monty. He felt the hairs on the back of his neck rise and any worry about observers fled his mind.

"Is this manner of dress sufficient?" asked Rodin, taking a step back to present himself.

"Umm. Oh," Monty stumbled over his words. "Yes. Yes, quite sufficient indeed."

Rodin cocked his head and listened.

"Music," he whispered.

He grabbed Monty by the hand and pulled him into the room. Rodin headed towards the pianist who still played the Boston. Rodin listened and watched the two young women who were making their way through the steps. He studied them for a moment, and then turned to Monty. He took the cocktail glass from Monty's hand, placed it on the piano and said, "Come."

He pulled Monty very close and positioned them to match the young ladies' formation. Monty was so shocked he let himself be led without thinking. They began to make the steps of the dance and moved around in a circular formation, just near the young ladies. Monty had never danced the Boston before but it didn't seem so very different from a number of waltzes he had learned in his years, the step only seemed abbreviated.

As they settled into a mutual rhythm, a sense of embarrassment began to wash over Monty. He was acutely aware of being in a private home and that he was surrounded by people. Surely he had stolen a moment or two like this, deep in the darkened recesses of a club in Paris, or at the Brunswick on his few trips there. But those places were made for the kind of company kept who also partook in such dances. Anywhere else they would have been thought unseemly, scandalous. It was all well and good for two unattached young ladies to partner in the absence of a male suitor, but for two men

whirling about a corner of the room like some per-
verse Regency ball was unheard of.

"Do you think we ought to be doing this?" he whispered as Rodin pulled him close.

"Why not?" asked Rodin. "No one seems to mind."

And as Rodin turned him into a spin, and Monty
lifted his arms, his eyes whirled around the room.
Rodin was right; the only ones bothering to even
watch them seemed to be enjoying the sight. He
even caught sight of Bishop smiling broadly and
Jodhpurs looking on with wide-eyed amusement.
Monty smiled back and closed his eyes as he fin-
ished his spin and was pulled nearer to Rodin
again. Silently, Monty thanked Aunt Charlotte for
her choice of friends and relished the novel sense
of freedom.

Trevor would have been absolutely apoplectic at
the mere suggestion of such an abandonment of
propriety. Being so familiar with another man in
front of a crowd, of mixed company at that. Trevor
simply would have withered away. But why did that
come to mind now? Monty chastised himself. Con-
stantly these thoughts of Paris, which he had pushed
aside for so long now, threatened to invade. He did
not want to think of Trevor now, or any of that.

As if on cue, Rodin tightened the grip of his hand
on Monty's waist.

"What are you thinking of?" he whispered.

Monty opened his eyes and gazed into those tender pools of brown.

"Nothing," he replied. "Nothing except this moment. And how good it feels."

"Good." Rodin nodded and they continued to dance.

The pianist stretched the number quite longer than its usual time and mixed in differing tempos as well. Others were inspired by their obvious enjoyment of the music and, in not too long a time, a small crowd of dancers filled the half of the room near the piano. The young player started a new song, which Monty did not at all recognize, whose syncopation felt brand new. Some of the ragtime he had heard mentioned, he imagined.

Although none of the crowd knew any particular steps, they did the best they could and bobbed along with much good charm. Rodin seemed to adjust easily to the new rhythm. He interlocked his arms with one point, and even began a movement whereby he lifted his knees and did a bit of a hop. It was slightly ridiculous, but it seemed to fit the music perfectly, and Monty had to admit, was rather a fetching display of the body. Many of the crowd soon mimicked Rodin and began a bit of hopping as well. Monty was overcome by the giddiness of it and burst into laughter, enjoying it and devoting himself to the animal-like dances.

After countless minutes of this, Monty patted Rodin on the chest, signaling that he needed a short break. He dashed over to the drinks tray and prepared drinks for himself and his dance partner. He was exhilarated by the music and movement, and found himself quite glad that he was having a moment alone with Rodin, uninterrupted by worry and suspicion.

Bishop tapped him on the shoulder.

"If you're quite through with your experimental movements, oughtn't we head to the Brunswick? It's getting rather late."

Monty took a great sip of his drink and poured more into the glass. He felt annoyance at his friend's presence in an unusual way.

"I thought you were busy with Old Jodhpurs?"

"Oh." Bishop sighed. "He was as boring as all that Russian poetry you so loved. I abandoned him in the cards room. I think we ought to make for the Brunswick; it's starting to pale here."

"No," Monty declared quite forcefully, surprising even himself. "I'm not ready yet."

Bishop raised his brows. "How much longer then?"

"I'll let you know," said Monty. He grabbed the two cocktails and stalked past Bishop.

"Monty," Bishop called after him but he ignored his friend.

Monty returned to Rodin who was watching the dancers and bobbing his head to the music. Monty pressed a glass into his hand.

"Come with me now, please," he said, grabbing Rodin's hand and leading him towards the back of the room.

They neared a bookshelf and Monty peered at its shelves.

"Ah," he said and reached up.

He grabbed one of the books there, pulling it down from the top of its spine. There was a clicking sound and one portion of the bookshelf popped out from the rest slightly. Monty pressed his fingers into the crack and pried open the secret door. Rodin looked delighted.

"Come, come," Monty whispered and he slid through the doorway.

Rodin followed and they found themselves in a room that resembled a study. All around them were shelves filled with books, with a large desk to one side, on the front side of the house, just under a window. There was a large globe in one corner of the room, along with many artifacts and bibelots whose styles were incongruous enough to suggest a personal collection. The two sofas and the chairs scattered about the room were covered in dust sheets.

"This was Bishop's grandfather's study," explained Monty. "Bishop and I used to escape back here many times when I would visit and he could no longer cope with his parents. They keep it open when they are in residence, but no one uses it."

He whipped a dust sheet from one of the sofas and flung it on top of a nearby chair.

"There's another exit just there."

Monty pointed to a slim panel of the wall on the opposite side of the room that had a fresco painted on it to resemble a pergola in an overgrown garden.

"Where does it lead?" asked Rodin.

"If you follow the short passage, it comes out just behind the stairwell in the main foyer."

"This house has secrets," said Rodin.

"Don't they all?" Monty dropped onto the sofa. He took a gulp of his drink. "Where did you learn to dance like that?"

Rodin settled onto the sofa opposite Monty.

"Some of that I had seen before. The rest, I only let my body do what felt proper in the moment."

"I'm not quite sure many would call what our bodies were doing out there 'proper.'"

Rodin shook his head, smiling. "Then they must learn to trust themselves more. Our bodies often tell us what they need as much as what they want. Why should we deny either? I have seen many rules that have stopped people from being what they are, and it does no good in the end."

Monty nodded. "Bishop said something like that earlier. More or less."

"You seem very different from Bishop," said Rodin. "You have been friends for a very long time?"

"Since we were boys." He too put his cocktail down. "Different? Yes. I suppose so. I'm not aristocracy, of course if that's what you mean. My father was only a businessman. A very successful merchant who married a white woman of minor connection—but her place in society gave him entree. They were all great snobs, of course, and though they looked down on him for being nouveau riche, and Indian to boot, but, in the end, there's little they love more than money. So, despite their feelings, they invited him into their drawing rooms."

"Not drawing rooms like these," said Rodin.

Monty laughed. "No, indeed not."

He picked up his glass and drained it.

"Do you know," he continued, "my family name was originally Singh but Father changed it when he first moved to London. He said he wanted to sound more acceptable."

"Did this work?"

Monty shrugged. "In the end, he still had to donate an enormous sum to get me into Eton, despite my being the cleverest chap in my class. But, of course, being clever never means much. Not to those types of people, anyway. They only see what matters to them.

"It didn't matter much to me, really. I always felt like an outsider, as if I didn't belong, even in the places where nobody thought I belonged anywhere else."

"In the many places I have been, it has been my experience that people do not value the ones they should. They often shun the most magnificent stars in the night sky, so that they do not shine too brightly over the others."

"That's awfully poetic."

Rodin moved closer to Monty on the sofa. "Poetry and truth are hard to separate."

"Where did you learn that?"

"I have seen many things. And I have traveled many places."

Monty studied the handsome face before him. His strong jaw, his full lips, the powerful neck, whose lines stretched long as Rodin tilted his head. "And what have you learned from this education of the world?"

Rodin leaned in closely. "I have learned to trust my heart."

He opened his mouth for a kiss but Monty held up his hands, pushing him back. He leveled Rodin with a look. "What are you?"

Rodin was surprised. "What do you mean? You know what I am."

"No, but I mean where did you come from? How do you become what you are?" Monty pressed his fingers to his temples. "Did I somehow manifest you? Is it possible that I somehow created you? Are you, in fact, real?"

Rodin gave him a bemused smile and shook his head. "Of course I am real."

"But how? How is it possible I have seen you in my mind all these years? And yet I've never met you."

"Because we know each other."

Monty shook his head, frowning. "But we do not. Not before today."

Rodin reached over and took Monty's hands. He brought them to Monty's lap and held them there. His touch was soothing and despite his confusion, Monty felt calmed.

"We do not know each other in the way that you mean, no. But our fates have been tied already."

"What does that mean, Rodin? Why do you insist on talking in riddles?"

"These are not riddles I speak, but truth."

"You just said that the truth was poetry. And poetry is full of riddles."

Rodin smiled and brought Monty's hand to his lips, kissing the back of it. "This is quite true."

The same sensation swept over Monty as before. He felt a pulling, a tugging at his center, that made him want to press himself against Rodin. Breathe him in and kiss his neck as he kissed Monty's hand. But still he resisted.

"What is your real name?" Monty asked. He felt as if he must know all about this strange man.

"Rodin will do."

"But you must have a name before that, surely."

"Yes. It is hard for you to understand, my name before. I will tell it to you one day. But now I like the name you have chosen for me. I like that it comes from you."

"But why me?"

"Why not you?"

Monty moved closer to Rodin, and Rodin's grip on his hands tightened.

"Where did you come from before?" asked Monty. "Before you were here, I mean. Before we found you."

"Before you found me," Rodin repeated, his eyes sparkling. "For a long time I was in France. But then I came here."

Monty was surprised at that. "France? Really?"

"Yes."

"But that's extraordinary."

"Many things in life are extraordinary if you see them correctly."

Monty looked at him, a new insight dawning within him. One he was too hesitant to believe just yet.

"Did it take you very long to get here?"

"To get to the lake, yes. Too long. I was sad and felt I might be lost, that my search was in vain."

"How long did it take you?"

"Since Paris," said Rodin.

"But when was Paris?"

Rodin shook his head. "I do not know time in the way that you do. I cannot say. Only since Paris."

"So," Monty began. "What were you searching for? Why did you come here?"

Rodin caressed Monty's cheek. "But you know why. You must."

"How could I know why?"

"Because," said Rodin. "I came here for you."

He kissed Monty.

It was a kiss like none other Monty had ever experienced. He felt Rodin's tongue in his mouth, luscious and soft yet penetrating. He took Monty's mouth with his own, and all sensation crashed into one current. In his ears, Monty thought he heard the sound of the sea rushing in. His body felt completely relaxed but at the same time urgent, as if he wanted to wrap all of his limbs around the man kissing him and dragging him to the floor. He used both of his hands to clasp Rodin's face, pulling his mouth harder against his own. His mouth was sweet, like the tang of the cocktail, but also salty, deeply salty like the sea or tears.

He heard himself moan slightly, the sound reverberating in both their mouths. He might have felt silly for this, but it encouraged Rodin. He tugged Monty tight against him; Monty wrapped his arms around Rodin's neck. Rodin reclined so that the full weight of Monty's body rested on his. He gripped Monty by the back of the head and pulled his mouth away, instead kissing his neck, nuzzling his ears, and then softly letting his lips touch Monty's forehead.

Their breathing came to a lull, and Monty lay against his chest. He wasn't sure if it was the cocktails or the headiness of the kiss he had resisted for so long, but his head was swimming, as if he had been submerged. And yet he could breathe. The blood coursed through him, he could feel every pulse of it, and his breath filled his lungs, bringing a placid feeling. He rested his hand on Rodin's bicep, caressing it through the material.

Rodin picked up his hand, kissing the fingers, and then interlocked them with his own.

"I'm not sure I understand any of this," Monty whispered.

Rodin lifted his face, pulling it close to his own.

"Do you understand this?" he asked, and kissed Monty again.

He might have drunk a vial of laudanum for the giddiness he felt when Rodin released his mouth.

"Yes," he said, his eyes closed. "I do understand that."

"Then that is all you need," Rodin assured him.

"There you are! I might have known!" Bishop came barreling through the hidden door panel they had entered. "I should have come here first. I should have known you were in our old hiding place, Monty. But, not time for that, chaps, we've got to get moving."

Pearson followed Bishop into the room.

"But Bishop—" Monty began to protest.

"Not now, Monty. We must escape before that bloody American shackles Pearson to the card table all night."

"The card table is not where I worry about him shackling me," said Pearson.

"Quick, quick!" cried Bishop. "Your coats are by the front door. Oh, bugger! We don't have a coat for Rodin."

"I do not need a coat."

"Yes, fine. Then make haste, both of you."

Bishop waved his hands, ushering them, like lost sheep, to the other hidden entrance.

"There's a cab that's been waiting outside while I searched for you. Soon it will be carriages at eleven and we'll lose him to the theater crowd."

Monty was about to object again, but as they entered the passageway behind the second hidden door, the depth of the darkness hushed him. He stuck out his hand in front of him and he felt Rodin grab it.

"Don't mind the darkness," said Bishop. "Just keep straight."

"Weren't there lights here before?" asked Monty.

"There are barely enough servants to stoke the furnace, Monty. You can't expect them to be lighting every lamp in every nook and crevice. Especially hidden rooms no one would expect to use, you dirty rascals."

They paused as Bishop pushed on something, something that Monty still could not see, and a panel popped open in front of them, light streaming in. They were in the main foyer.

"There we are," cried Bishop. He darted ahead and grabbed the coats and hats.

As Rodin and Monty rounded the end of the staircase, with Pearson just behind, Aunt Charlotte emerged from the card room.

"So you are going to your club then, after all?" she asked.

"Slowly but surely," said Bishop.

He shoved the hats and coats into his friend's hands.

"I imagine you'll all be out to all hours," said Aunt Charlotte as she followed them to the door. "But we will have a grand breakfast buffet, as always. So do try to be back in time for that. I know you will enjoy it, and there will be so much to talk about. Mister Herald has been asking me all sorts of questions about you all evening. And, too, I always find that the more half-drunk young men there are of a morning meal, the more interestingly it goes."

Rodin paused.

"Will there be kippers?" asked Rodin.

"Yes, of course," said Aunt Charlotte. "Deviled kidneys, kedgeree, and the whole lot. Breakfast, you know, is my favorite meal. I like to start my day with an intention."

Rodin nodded. "Kippers are my favorite."

Monty couldn't help but guffaw. Bishop rolled his eyes.

"Of course they are," said Bishop dryly, tugging on his sleeve to get him moving again.

"Then I shall endeavor to have jugs and jugs of kippers," said Aunt Charlotte. "I can tell you are a man of healthy appetite."

"Yes, that's lovely," Bishop shoved his two companions out the front door. "Three for kippers and kedgeree dear Aunt, we shan't forget."

"Must you go? Won't your club be rather dull at this late hour?"

"Not that usual sort of club, Aunt. It's more of a cabaret theatre club—I believe some have referred to them as night clubs. It's a fairly novel thing, you know."

"I say," said Aunt Charlotte, her interest piqued. "How very European of you."

"Yes, it is, rather."

Bishop kissed his aunt on the cheek, ready to dash.

Anderson Herald popped out of the drawing room, his head swiveling.

"Charlotte, there you are! And Mister Pearson! You must come back quickly. I am convinced these two bridge partners you have us playing against can give each other signals through some sort of thought-reading or something. Is it possible they know magic?"

"Don't be ridiculous, Anderson. Magic doesn't exist."

"I don't know. Back home there was a woman who claimed to have resurrected her grandmother from the grave. And together the both of them were able to hypnotize their entire town to do their bidding."

Charlotte clasped his hand and guided him back towards the blue drawing room.

"Well, yes, of course, dear. I don't doubt that happened. But, you see, that is America; Americans are far more suggestible."

"If you say so."

"I do."

She turned back towards the departing men. "Oh, but Mister Pearson. What are we to do about the cards?"

"I believe I saw a woman giving tarot in the front parlour," responded Bishop. "Maybe she can help you. Goodnight, Aunt Charlotte!"

Chapter Nine

Paris, 1907

T he conversation of the crowd was like a sea of noise below. It was similar to standing in the train station waiting for an approaching train. Everyone felt the need to say all they could say before the signal ended their chance, as if, not long after they would not have all the time they needed to speak again. Here, too, they rushed to share all the details they possessed about what was about to happen, all the bits of gossip that had flown around—about those involved in the happening and those who spread the rumors. They exclaimed at a friend unseen in months, boasted as to who had been here last recently and judged those who never came. The opera house was alive with chatter, and Monty loved looking down at the wash of people. Here, unlike the train station with its drab traveling clothes and sad overtones of goodbye, the crowd was awash in color and buoyed by cheerful expectation. All the best silks flashed vibrant in their gowns and waistcoats, the earrings and necklaces and tiaras and cufflinks glistened more brightly than the chandeliers that lit them. Seeing the crowd proved almost as magical as anything that might happen onstage.

"I'm not sure which you enjoy more, the opera or the opera goers," said Trevor, amused.

Monty leaned back from the edge of their box and into his seat. He smiled at his lover.

"It's true," he said. "It's still very new and magical for me, I suppose. These kinds of experiences were rare for me as a child."

"Had they not been, you might have grown bored of them very early in life."

Monty frowned. "Is it too awful to sit through another? I appreciate you coming, I know how little you care for it."

"Not at all. I find your enthusiasm more than charming. And I wanted a chance to experience this with you one time."

"We'll have plenty of chances back home as well. Bishop has a reserved box he hardly ever uses. And I plan to keep his seat warm for him."

Trevor gave him a look then, at once warm yet somehow distant. As a photographer might study the composition of a family portrait.

"Yes, of course," Trevor said. "Did you bring the new opera glasses I got for you?"

"Of course," Monty exclaimed.

They folded up quite small and he had stashed them in the interior pocket of his jacket. He retrieved them now and held them to his face, scanning various parts of the opera house to test their magnification.

Scanning directly across from their box, on the opposite side, he came to a stop.

"I'll be damned," he said.

"Is something the matter? Don't they work correctly?"

"Oh, no, the glasses are fine. But it's Bishop."

"Bishop?"

"Yes, in the box across from us, just to the left. That's very odd. I mentioned to him that we were coming earlier this week, and he said nothing."

Monty was surprised. Even when Trevor came along to the theatre, if Bishop was interested they always sat together. Why would he have avoided them tonight? But then he saw what he thought was the answer.

"It seems he is here with someone," said Trevor. "Anyone we know, or another of Bishop's new conquests?"

"Uncle Freddy," Monty said flatly.

Trevor looked up from the programme he was studying.

"That damned German chap once more? I didn't realize he was so very much in the picture again."

"I haven't heard mention of him since that night of the cabaret," agreed Monty.

Monty could not help but continue to watch them. They seemed to be in a heated, if hushed, conversation and Bishop's face was creased with anxiety—and, too, Monty thought, fear. Friedrich was turned away from Monty's view, but he could see that he was leaning into Bishop, clearly unhappy with him, his shoulders tight and hunched. Bishop kept moving back into his chair until it appeared as if he were trying to push himself into its cushioned frame. He was nodding his head furiously and uttering one or two word replies to whatever words Friedrich was saying to him. Monty was convinced he was afraid to say more. Then, abruptly, Friedrich grabbed Bishop roughly by the wrist and pulled him forward in his seat. The house lights dimmed just then indicating that the opera would begin shortly, and Bishop's gaze jerked away from Friedrich for just a moment.

Monty raised his hand then, trying to signal to his friend. He hoped that if he could let Bishop know he was nearby he might be able to extricate himself from the box with Friedrich and come sit with them. Bishop caught the movement and looked Monty's way. He recognized his friend behind the opera glasses but he did not wave in reply. Instead, he gave what was an almost imperceptible shake of the head. Just then the house lights started to dim. Friedrich noticed the small movement and his head jerked over his shoulder, peering in Monty's direction.

Friedrich's eyes seemed to glow like hot, red coals in the dim light and Monty gasped. Undone and frightened by what he saw, he snatched the opera glasses away from his face and turned towards the stage.

Trevor placed his hand over Monty's. "Is everything all right?"

"Yes. No. Well, I'm not entirely sure, actually."

The orchestra began to play and Monty shook his head, trying to clear it of the momentary fright he'd

felt. He gave Trevor a wan smile and studied the
stage, though, in truth, he was not concentrating on
the action.

What a bizarre thing, he thought to himself. How
could his eyes glow? Surely it was a trick of the lights
reflecting from the stage somehow? Or a reflection
within his opera glasses as the torches dimmed? He
remembered the night at the Cabaret l'Enfer and
how Friedrich's pipe had glowed preternaturally
bright. Maybe he was overlapping the two moments
in his mind. Maybe he was seeing what he expected
to see, what he had conjured in his mind. Some
sort of projection of his dislike for the man made
him see things. It was the only plausible explanation,
really.

Monty tried to concentrate on the scene unfolding
onstage, tried to lose himself in the music as he
usually so easily did. After a few minutes, his opera
glasses turned towards the stage, he dared to sneak
a view in the direction of Bishop's box. He did not
linger but from what he could see, there seemed to
be calm. Both sat back in their seats watching the
performance, and there were no glowing eyes to be
seen. Bishop did, however, seem stiff: sitting straight
in his chair, his neck frozen as if he dared not look
in any direction but forward. It was not as jolly a
scene as Monty might have hoped, but all seemed
free from great tension for the time being.

The opera was engrossing and Monty did manage
to get swept away by the music. So much so that
most of the first act had passed before he thought
to check in on his friend again. He leaned back,

ostensibly to stretch his neck, and let his glasses casually scan past Bishop's box. He jerked his head back. The box was empty; they were gone. Worry filled him and he began to wonder how long they had been gone. Were they still at the opera house? Had the scene become even more ferocious?

He was up out of his seat before he realized and heading out of the box. Trevor caught him by the sleeve.

"Where are you going?" he whispered.

"Shan't be a tick," Monty whispered back, trying to sound reassuring.

He made his way out onto the foyer, in search. A movement out of the corner of his eye caught his attention. In the direction of the bar, there was an alcove to the side that seemed to be curtained off. The curtain moved in rough jerks, suggesting there was motion behind it. Monty hoped he wasn't disturbing some young couple's secret moment but, all the same, he dashed towards the alcove and pulled back the curtain. Even as he did so, he noted a strange noise, something like the growl of a dog mixed with the churn of machinery. He didn't have time to register what the noise could possibly be, for as he pulled the material aside, he saw what he had feared.

Bishop was backed—no, pressed—into the back of the alcove, with Friedrich glowering over him, threatening. Bishop had a drop of blood at his mouth, where it appeared he had a broken lip, and Friedrich's hand was around his throat. Underneath where Friedrich's hand pressed into his flesh, there were bruises, livid and dark. Monty, in anger, punched Friedrich in the shoulder.

"What the hell are you doing?" he cried.

Friedrich turned on him suddenly and growled a warning. As he did his face seemed to almost shift in shape, becoming near monstrous. With his free arm, he pushed Monty hard and Monty stumbled back. He almost fell to the floor, but he caught himself. When he looked up again, Friedrich's face appeared perfectly normal though still he glared.

"Go away, you fool," Friedrich growled at him.

"I will not leave my friend like this," Monty countered.

"It's all right, Monty," said Bishop, his voice strained. "Really it is. Freddy and I were just having a little quarrel that got out of hand. You know what we men can be like."

"Bishop, are you sure? This seems nothing like a small quarrel."

"What it is," snapped Friedrich, his voice returned to a normal tone, "is none of your concern. I suggest you mind your affairs. Your friend is man enough to settle his own agreements."

Agreements?

Friedrich had released his grip on Bishop and they both began to back out of the alcove. Bishop brought a handkerchief to his mouth, and tugged at his collar, trying to put it up farther. Monty moved toward him, but Friedrich stepped forward and between them. Monty bumped into the man and almost stumbled backward again. Though he didn't seem so, Friedrich was more than solidly built, and Monty didn't think he could move him if he tried.

Inside, he heard applause signaling the end of Act One.

"As I said," Friedrich said, "we will continue our conversation in private, as intended."

"Bishop, are you quite sure?"

Bishop nodded, his voice much stronger now. "Leave us be, Monty. Don't concern yourself with my affairs."

People had started milling out for the interval. Monty did not believe that things were at all all right but he wasn't sure how he could make any difference if his friend insisted on being so stubborn. He opened his mouth to speak but was interrupted.

"Mister Singer?" A warm female voice called out. "Montgomery, is that you?"

He turned to see who was calling him, and then turned back. And, in just that snip of time, Bishop and Friedrich were gone.

"I didn't know you would be here tonight."

"Good evening, Mademoiselle Lazevski. What a delight," Monty answered with forced cheeriness.

They both moved forward through the crowd and met halfway.

"Are you quite all right, my friend?" she asked. "You look a bit shaken."

"Yes, well, you know how I am at the opera or the theatre. I get carried away. But you, look at you, you look stunning. Like a princess."

Selika Lazevski waved away his compliment, but it was earnestly meant. Monty most often saw her in the *tenue sober* of dressage riding kit. Her jacket and skirt were almost the same shade of brown as her skin, so that she looked like some grand Roman warrior carved out of marble, or a goddess armored from head to toe. She was always the picture of the formidable horsewoman who was famous throughout France for riding *haute école*.

But tonight she wore a sumptuous green gown with matching jewels at the ears and neck, and, instead of her usual top hat, her hair was piled on top of her head and adorned with a sparkling headband with feathers springing from its side, themselves made out of multi-colored crystals. She was a picture.

"Good lord, is that you, Selika?" Trevor approached them both.

"Lord Mawnton," cried Selika with a broad smile. "I have found two treasures tonight. How lovely to see you."

"None of that now," said Trevor. "No lords and ladies tonight. Let's have one evening of just being ourselves, not our titles."

"Of course," she said with a nod.

"I was just telling our lovely friend how much she resembles a princess this evening," added Monty, trying to re-establish a normal feeling, after the stirred emotions of the encounter with Bishop.

"Montgomery flatters me, and I'll have none of it," she said with a small laugh.

"His flattery is more than correct," said Trevor grandly. "Are you enjoying the opera?"

"Indeed I am, most assuredly. Though maybe not quite as much as your friend Montgomery. He was just telling me how the emotion had moved him so."

Trevor eyed Monty. "Yes, he is often overtaken by emotion."

"Which box are you in?" asked Monty.

"Oh, no, I'm in the orchestra."

"Nonsense," said Monty. "You must join us in our box. There's more than room enough, and I can show you the new pair of opera glasses Trevor gifted me with."

"How kind of you, and, of course, I shall accept your invitation gladly. And I hope you allow me to extend my own. There are a good number of us meeting at Maxim's for a late supper after the opera. Won't you join us?"

"Oh, that would be—" began Monty.

"I'm afraid we cannot join you this evening," Trevor said hastily and with heft. "We have other plans after."

Monty was confused but smiled, playing along. He knew of no plans and Trevor typically liked a large supper party to get lost in, especially after the theatre. If nothing else than to give him respite from Monty's commentary and endless chatter about a production he had not enjoyed.

"Of course, I understand," said Selika graciously. "But seeing as I now have the escort of two such fine gentleman, won't you join me in a glass of champagne before we return to our seats?"

"*Avec plaisir,*" said Trevor as he extended his arm.

They walked for quite some time after leaving the
opera house, a tense silence between them. Trevor
had something on his mind, but Monty knew not
whether it troubled his mind or simply distracted
him. Either way, he was hesitant to provoke explo-
ration. Monty brought them to a stop in their walk
just by the *Fontaine des Mers*, a particular favorite of
his.

   The last time he recalled visiting the Place de
la Concorde was to watch the *Mi-Carême* proces-
sion earlier in the year. Bishop had word that an
artist friend of a friend would be at the *Carnaval*
to document the event on a motion picture machine. Such a change from that day, the plaza was
almost empty tonight, not swarmed by people as
it had been during the celebration when he could
hardly lift his arms in either direction, much less
study the founts. They had watched as the camera
focused in on and followed one enormous float on
the top of which was the grotesque head of a giant,
its tongue lolling out, and a knife in its hand. It had
not meant to be frightening, but thinking back on it
now, Monty shivered. For some reason, his memory
transplanted the angry visage of Friedrich onto the
creature. How he had been earlier at the opera this
evening—his eyes wide and full of rage, his mouth
agape almost as if his teeth were bared, and his face
livid and flushed. He would have made a perfect

gargoyle, carved into stone. He sincerely hoped his friend was okay. The scene behind the curtain with Friedrich was not reassuring at all.

"The French do love their gold," commented Trevor, breaking the silence.

"And bronze," said Monty. "But I believe it is all paint now."

"Are they meant to be mermaids or something?"

Monty looked up at one of the great statues which lined the outer rim of the fountain. She was turned away from him, her face lifted toward the sky. The bronzed fish she held in her arm shot a great arc of water from its mouth up and behind, covering her crown of shells and coral in a fine mist.

"This is a sea nymph," Monty explained. "A nereid in mythology. Kind creatures that helped sailors navigate and survive the storms."

Trevor looked up and around at them. "Seems like a waste of water to have them running like this all the time."

"The water goes back into the Seine," said Monty. "So I suppose it isn't wasted."

He turned to Trevor.

"Is there something the matter, Trevor? Despite Selika's very kind invitation to dinner, you insisted we must go. As if there were something very important we must attend. But we have done nothing but walk in silence since the opera house."

Trevor dropped his gaze.

"I needed to talk with you tonight."

"Particularly tonight?"

"Yes, particularly tonight. You know, I must return to England in the next few days."

A familiar subject; Monty's chest expanded a bit, the tension easing a bit.

"Of course. We've talked about it many times. It won't be so long before Bishop and I, too, will be returning home. We will be reunited in not a very long time. Of course, I have to visit my family first before I can come see you but it shouldn't be a very long commitment of time—"

Trevor cleared his throat. "That's just it, Monty. I don't think we shall have a reunion—not of the kind you mean, at least."

Monty's chest again felt tight, as if a steel bar had suddenly been wound round it.

"What are you saying, Trevor?"

Trevor peered up at the fountain as if it could provide some insight for him. Maybe he thought himself some sailor, lost in a storm, Monty thought.

"This time in Paris with you was possibly the most exhilarating time of my life. I know you think I am grumpy and small-minded about many things, but, despite all of that, I have never felt such exuberance for things as I have when I've been with you."

He paused, but Monty had no words to fill the pause. He was frozen in dread.

"And while it has been a good time—perhaps the best of my life thus far—we both knew this could not last forever, that it could go no further than the limits of this fantastical city."

"Did we both?" Monty asked, his voice heavy. "I'm not sure that I knew that."

"Oh, Monty, you can't be that naïve, good lord. You had to have known somewhere, on some level that we could not just show up back in England tied together with some pretty ribbon as if we'd just returned from a honeymoon."

"I never said anything of the sort. I am not a fool, Trevor. Nor so naïve as you suggest, but I thought we had something deeper than a holiday tryst. The way we talked, the things you've shared with me, alone, just the two of us, in bed together, in my hotel room. Those are not things you discuss with an acquaintance or a prostitute or whatever you are trying to paint me as now."

Trevor balked at his words.

"Nothing like that at all. I have never held you in any such regard, you must know that. You intend to wound me."

Monty scoffed. "And what do you intend for me?"

"You can't be as shocked as that. Surely, you must have contemplated how this would end."

"I do not go into these things thinking about how they end."

Trevor sighed. "Then perhaps you are naïve."

"I beg your pardon?"

"Monty, be realistic. We have to think on our every step. Our every gesture, our every expression; who we associate ourselves with; the places we go. We are lucky if we can even contemplate an ending that doesn't involve scandal, or shunning, or jail time. There is no place in this world for us if you do not contemplate such things."

"Then perhaps this is not the world for me."

"Why should I expect you to understand?"

Monty turned to him then. "Why wouldn't I? What is so bizarre about my ability to understand?"

"Keep your voice down," hissed Trevor.

Just then a couple came near the fountain and Monty turned quickly back to watch the water shooting up into the air. On the other side of the fountain, just beside the plaza, a carriage went by. There was a woman inside, talking to a companion. Monty couldn't see to whom she was talking, but her face was lit up, laughter on her lips. She lifted her hand and pressed the flower she was holding close to her face, inhaling of its scent.

"I only mean that we come from different worlds inasmuch as I am expected to produce an heir," Trevor continued. "You cannot know that particular pressure."

"I think I can know the pressure of the expectation to be a regular, everyday man as much as the next. I may not be expected to sire a prize foal onto whom I must foist my legacy and title, but do not think that at every turn I, too, do not have the wonderings of parents and relatives and friends. Concerned if I am a normal man, with normal urges. And as it comes to the expectations of society, I think you'll find they bear little difference whether one has a goddamn title or not."

"There's no need to get snappish, Monty. I don't mean to insult you."

"No. Only to cast me aside."

Trevor took a step towards him, pointing.

"Hear, now. Are we to have histrionics? I have to do what I must and you know. Had I known I would have such scenes awaiting me, I might as well have taken a woman as a lover."

"Maybe you ought to have," snapped Monty. "Then, at least, you could have kept her on as a mistress."

Trevor cursed and walked away. He traipsed around in a small, tight circle, his fists clenched, and his eyes opening and shutting, fighting against the explosion of emotion clearly roiling inside. He came to a halt.

"Monty," he began, his voice softer than before, "I had hoped we could remain friends, as awkward and difficult as that might be at first. You act as if I want this. And I assure you, I do not. But what am I to do?"

Monty could not respond. They stood in silence for a moment.

Monty watched the water ripple within the bed of the fountain. He thought about him and Trevor as future friends. It was precious little but something within him grabbed a hold of the thread; despite good sense, he felt the need.

"I suppose all your time when you return will be taken up with finding a suitable wife. I imagine you will be coming back and forth from the city quite often?"

There was a deathly moment of silence. When Trevor next spoke, he sounded exhausted, his voice came as if from a great distance, weak and thin.

"I have already found a wife, Monty. I was engaged before I arrived in Paris."

The thread was snapped. Monty felt as if a dagger had been plunged into his chest and he resisted the urge to double over in pain.

"What?" he gasped.

"It was only supposed to be one summer in France," Trevor began.

Monty took several steps forward, his eyes on the water within the fountain. He moved towards it, yearning to feel its cooling touch. He stopped just at the edge, letting the mist from the spouting founts fall on his face. He hoped it covered the tears burning in his eyes.

He looked down at the water and part of him wished it was deep, deeper than a fountain, so deep without end.

"One summer and then back to England and on with the marriage," Trevor continued. He spoke in rote, telling of his past plans. As if any of it mattered now. "A last sowing of oats, I suppose. But then I met you, Monty." Here his voice faltered. "I-I didn't expect to meet someone who I would cherish so deeply, for whom I would have such immense feelings. So I put off my return under the pretense of making connections here in France that would benefit the family. My father understood, at first. But my return is overdue, questions are starting to be asked. If I delay it any further, I risk bringing not only shame to my family but my wife's family as well. They wonder if I intend to go through with it at this point."

"And do you wonder?

"Monty, I must. I have obligations."

"And what of your obligation to me?" Despite himself, Monty heard his voice crack.

"Stop it, Monty! Just stop. Please!"

Monty stepped away from the fountain, turning and walking a few paces away from Trevor. He stopped, unfolding his handkerchief and wiping the wetness from his face.

"You judge me for doing what's expected of me," Trevor said. "But what else can I do?"

"You can be the man you ought to be."

"I don't have that choice, Monty. If I abandon my responsibility my entire family can be ruined. I don't have the freedom that you, or even Bishop, have. Tromping along, enjoying life, letting its currents take you wherever they may wash up is exhilarating. But though for you it may be life, the whole and sum of it, for me it was only a tributary off the main course. And now I must steer myself back to the land, back to real life and its responsibilities."

"And where does that leave me? Some flotsam in the waters you've sailed past?" Monty asked. "Despite what you may call my histrionics, I am aware that I can never mean everything to you, but I thought maybe I would mean more than that."

"You do, of course."

"Only the rest of it matters more?"

"Yes. I wish it didn't. But yes."

Monty nodded, the hot tears threatening again. He bit his lip, trying to stop its trembling.

"Goodbye, Trevor," he finally croaked.

"It doesn't have to be like this. We can still be friends. I cannot say goodbye, Monty."

"Then I shall say it for both of us."

He left the plaza, his mind a blur. He did not know where he was going, only that his feet must move, must carry him forward, must carry him away.

In the distance he heard the sound of the river.

Chapter Ten

London, 1910

As an establishment of entertainment and leisure, *The Brunswick Dianthus* had not existed long. It was modeled after the cabaret and artist dens which existed mainly in Europe and other countries far less disapproving of Bohemia than England. It was intended as a cabaret and theatre club, each evening filled with various and varying spectacles of talent and the avant-garde, but what it became, more than anything, was a refuge for all the various and varying peoples of the city who had nowhere else to feel welcome. And, as luck would have it, these were usually the most talented and interesting of people as well, making it one of the most exciting spots in London.

It was headed by its inimitable and fierce pro-prietress Mrs. Frye, and her husband whose name no one knew and whom no one ever saw. She had converted the former basements of two for-mer millinery shops into a wide and long-stretching cave sunken below street level. Rumor had it that though everyone thought the pair of Fryes to be a married couple, from Lancashire or thereabouts, they were, in actual fact, brother and sister, but did little to discourage incorrect assumptions. They had found that suppliers and city authorities were more amenable to a respectable Mister and Missus than to liberal-minded siblings. And if talk held the seldom seen Mister to be slightly dubious politically and the Mrs. to be a little too well-dressed to be ladylike, their scads of inherited money helped to soften those rougher edges.

"Lord Brookesbay, I haven't seen you in quite some time," Mrs. Frye exclaimed as she met them near the entrance.

"Yes," said Bishop. "I've been spending more time in the country of late. You remember Mister Singer and Mister Pearson, of course, and this is our friend... well, he just likes to be called Rodin. One name, you know, just to keep things discreet."

Mrs. Frye studied Rodin's form.

"Of course, Rodin," she said. "My pleasure. I'll call them Victoria Lake, or whatever they please, if Bishop's got any more friends that look like you. Wonderful for business to have such fine-featured, well-heeled gentlemen about the place. The patrons love it. Shall I fetch you a table?"

"Yes, please. A large one; we're hoping to meet a few friends tonight."

She nodded. "I'll get you a proper-sized table then."

Towards the middle of the club, there was a stage. On the stage at their arrival was a young woman, demure in dress but painted rather theatrically. The piano clanked along perhaps a bit too loudly at times but fluently as she gave her best attempt at the music hall favorite 'The Boy I Love is Up in the Gallery'. She punctuated the song by pointing at various men throughout the cabaret and waving her handkerchief at them.

Rodin smiled at this and stepped forward a bit to get a better view. He listened, and then cocked his head to one side.

"The singer," he said. "She is a man."

"Yes, and she's rather flat," noted Bishop.

Just then the songstress tried, and failed, to hit a rather high note. The trio winced.

"You should sing for us," suggested Rodin. "The piano is sufficient."

Monty looked at Rodin questioningly; Bishop gazed out over the crowd.

"I don't sing anymore," Bishop answered, distracted.

"Not since Paris?" asked Rodin.

"Yes," Bishop said and then, realizing, turned around. "What in the deuce do you know about Paris? What has Monty told you?"

"I haven't told him anything," declared Monty. "I swear it."

"No, he did not tell me," said Rodin.

"Then how do you know about my singing?"

"I was there."

"Where?" asked Monty.

"In Paris. At the Café L'Enfer, the night you sang."

"I beg your pardon?" asked Bishop. "You were there? But how wcrc you— That is to say, were you there as yourself or as—how you appeared on the lake?"

"Is Rodin very fond of sailing?" asked Pearson.

"Not exactly," offered Monty.

"Gentlemen," announced Mrs. Frye, "I have a delightful table for you. Please, if you'll follow me."

"This is deuced queer," said Bishop, narrowing his eyes at Rodin.

"I am a little in the fog myself," added Monty.

"Are you?" asked Rodin, himself surprised. "But I explained to you."

"'Explained it to you'?" Bishop repeated. "Is that so, Monty?"

"I do hate to break up this little domestic squabble," said Pearson. "But go ahead and I'll join in a moment. I see someone I must speak with."

"Here we are," said Mrs. Frye as they approached the table.

Monty eyed the area she indicated.

"Must we be seated so near the draperies?" he asked.

"I'm sorry," said Mrs. Frye. "Do you not wish to be near the backrooms? That is Lord Brookesbay's usual preference."

"Yes, of course it is," replied Monty. "I'm hardly surprised."

"Dear Aunt Monty, your petticoats are showing again," said Bishop without looking back at him.

"What are the backrooms?" asked Rodin.

"Nothing you need concern yourself with."

Bishop gave a short laugh. "Rodin, my dear boy, he wants to keep you all to himself, you know. Don't go wandering off into the terrible unknown."

Monty glared at the back of Bishop's head but Rodin only smiled.

The waiter brought a carafe of wine and a tray of finger foods that fit the evening's theme—an Iberian mix of olives, almonds, and ham. Bishop was watching Rodin with a searching gaze. Rodin noticed and glanced back and forth between the two friends.

"Have I done something to offend?" he asked.

"I think we are both concerned with the fact that you haven't been entirely truthful with us," offered Monty.

"That is not the case. I have hidden nothing from you."

"I don't agree," countered Monty.

Just then a set of very familiar notes began to waft from the stage.

"Monty, wait. Quiet," whispered Bishop.

A light but flexible voice began to sing,

On a night my love strode the banks, by the waters opal black...

All three turned towards the source of the music, even Rodin who was making a study of the olives.

And talked to me of our hearts that might not ever be the same...

Monty studied the two young men onstage, the second waiting to sing harmony, was Pearson, and the lead he recognized as well.

"I'll be damned. Leggy," declared Monty.

"He does have the most marvelous knack for showing up, doesn't he? It's like he has some sixth sense when I'll be around."

"He is rather like a compass to your pole," agreed Monty.

Rodin refilled all of their wine glasses as they listened.

They had changed the arrangement somewhat, Monty noted. But that was not surprising as few could deftly manage the key changes that Bishop had composed.

And told me of our hearts and how we might ne'er get them back

They brought the song to a close with a shared harmony and a healthy amount of applause from the patrons.

"Thank you," said Leggy to the crowd. "That song was written by someone I like to think of as a dear friend. He is here tonight and I hope he won't mind our singing it. It's only the second time it's been sung in England."

They left the stage and made a beeline straight for the table.

"Do you gentleman mind if I join you?" asked Leggy.

"Yes, why not," said Bishop.

Bishop was trying to play it cool, as was so often his way when Leggy was around, but Monty knew he was moved. The pair had gotten closer than ever after that night in the cabaret in Paris, practically inseparable, but then something had happened. When Monty had tried to inquire, Bishop became snappish and trotted out his usual alibi of the future of two men having love, but Monty did not buy it. He suspected the sudden end had something more to do with the treacherous association with Friedrich, but he had known better than to even suggest that. Then, of course, with the way things had ended with Trevor, Bishop had felt even more justified in trotting out his excuse, pointing out to Monty how he himself had fallen afoul and proved himself a fool pursuing such fantasies.

Monty closed his eyes against that thought, not wanting to revisit it. When he opened them again, he found Rodin studying him. Rodin reached over and clasped his hand, giving it a tender squeeze. The threatening unease of Monty's memories dissipated.

Leggy, of course, took the seat nearest Bishop and sat as close as propriety would allow, even the propriety of an establishment such as this.

"Very good singing," said Rodin.

Leggy was anxious. "You didn't mind us singing your song, did you, Bishop?"

"It certainly got my attention."

"Yes," suggested Pearson, "I rather thought Nevin's *Narcissus* might be more in order, but Reginald insisted."

"Such wit!" cried Bishop, in a mocking tone. "Pray tell, what book did you steal that from, dear Pearson?"

Pearson gave him a sly look. "Had I, I'm sure it was not one you'd have read. No yellow-covered paperback."

"Ah, an aesthete. One borrowed from your lovely former gardener, no doubt.

Leggy turned to Pearson. "Yes, I was very sorrowful to hear about you and Jonas. I thought you were so comfortable together. In fact, I envied you."

Pearson raised his brows and took a strong sip.

"With my playing the secretary or the valet or the nursemaid or any such thing when unknown visitors came by? Envy is not warranted, I promise you."

Leggy nodded. "Understood. But there are certain concessions we must make, those of us akin, to have such a thing as domesticity in this world."

Pearson's frosty persona waned a bit. "Of course. Truly, I didn't really mind all that. But for the last long bit, we'd felt more like brothers than anything more. And while I know he cared for me, I don't think it would have ever gotten any deeper."

"Most fires burn to ashes eventually," added Bishop.

"Not all fires," said Leggy. "Some fires burn for a long while."

Bishop was surprised by this and Leggy glanced off nervously, concerning himself with pouring a glass of wine. Pearson caught Bishop's gaze and tilted his head.

"So long as the fire is properly stoked," Pearson said. "And the person feeding it isn't too irresponsible with the embers. Care must be taken with such things. Wouldn't you say, Bishop?"

"I've never had much skill for matters of housekeeping," said Bishop, averting his eyes.

"No," said Pearson. "But such skills can be learned." He turned to Monty. "Now, Mister Singer, introduce your new friend."

"Leggy, this is our friend Rodin, visiting from France."

"Visiting from France, you say," said Leggy. "Did you meet Mister Rodin during your time in Paris?"

"That seems to be very much the question of the evening," said Pearson.

"I saw Bishop and Monty at the cabaret," Rodin explained. "On the night when Bishop first performed the song you just sang."

"Unfortunately we didn't see him there," said Bishop.

Rodin turned to Monty. "No, but I saw you."

Pearson raised a brow and studied them.

"I remember it well. It was a magical night," Leggy said. "In some ways, when I think on it now, the performance feels like a dream."

Leggy was staring at Bishop as he said these words, but Bishop squinted at Rodin.

"Hear, now," said Bishop, the wine giving him quite a bit of gumption. "I feel far too little has been made of this coincidence of you being in Paris at the same time as us."

"I had been in Paris a very long time before you came," said Rodin. "Hardly a coincidence."

"But I thought that was how you all knew each other to begin with," said Pearson.

"Give me a cigarette, Pearson," said Bishop.

Bishop lit the fag and turned back to Rodin. "You mean to say that you were at the Café L'Enfer the night I sang and then you just so happened to appear in the lake on my family's property?"

"Again with this lake business," said Pearson. "I should think you're all obsessed with aquatics."

"So we were all at the L'Enfer on the same night?" asked Leggy. "That's rather a funny coincidence, isn't it?"

"Yes, exactly, Leggy!" cried Bishop. "I think there must be more to it in than just mere happenstance."

"Whoever asserted there was not?" asked Rodin, quite plainly.

"Why you sneaky little bugger," Bishop said. "Then ending up in my lake wasn't a mistake after all, was it?"

"No," answered Rodin without removing his gaze from Monty.

"Look, here," snapped Bishop. "What do you know of my arrangement in Paris? How are you involved?"

Rodin blinked. "Your 'arrangement'? I am at a loss."

"Would this arrangement, as you call it, be the reason you're so eager to seek out Weaver?" asked Monty.

Bishop flashed him a look and then peered down at the table. He smashed his cigarette into a plate. "Yes. Well, obviously, Monty."

"Not that tiresome centenarian again." Pearson sighed.

"A century old?" asked Rodin. "What is this man?"

Pearson shrugged. "What is any aristocrat?"

Leggy made a noise of objection. Pearson retrieved a cigarette from his case and lit it.

"Of course, I don't believe that he is strictly an aristocrat," Pearson continued with an eye roll. "But he was given an enormous pile of bricks by Lord Leighton—Grannus House. Actually, the story goes he was sold the house not given it. For a guinea, some decades ago, so that the family could not take it from Weaver once Leighton passed."

"He died?" asked Rodin.

"Yes, but they were companions," said Pearson, a knowing expression on his face. "Lifelong companions. Malcolm passed away some years ago and Weaver was as grey as a badger then. Where his fortune comes from, I couldn't say, naturally. But he has no want for anything."

"And they lived together, in this Grannus House, for all their lives?" Rodin leaned forward as he asked this.

"For as long as anyone can remember," confirmed Pearson. "They came to the city quite often, but there never seemed to be any scandal surrounding them. I've heard certain people, in jest, refer to them as our very own Ladies of Llangollen."

"To *certain* people." Bishop raised his wine glass.

Pearson inhaled deeply of his cigarette and blew a cloud of smoke in Bishop's direction.

"Yes, I would like to very much meet this man, after all," said Rodin. "Maybe he will let us visit this Grannus House."

Monty was confused by this.

"Are you very much interested in grand homes?" asked Monty.

"Possibly just the grounds and *lakes* surrounding them," suggested Bishop dryly.

"I would like to see the house where these two companions lived for so long. I would like to go there with you."

"With me?" asked Monty, surprised.

"You wouldn't be disappointed. It's a grand place," said Pearson. "Jonas did some work on the estate once—designing a garden for them—and Weaver invited us to one of his dinner parties. He's known for them."

"Speaking of dinners," interjected Bishop. "Let's get some food, shall we?"

Pearson exhaled a weary puff of smoke. "And more wine."

"And champagne," chimed in a broadly smiling Rodin.

Bishop raised his brows. "You heard the man. Champagne! But I'm afraid, my dear French friend, that they may not have kippers."

"Kippers?" said Leggy. "At this hour?"

Rodin leveled Bishop with a look. "Such wit," he said. "Did you acquire it from a book?"

Bishop guffawed.

"Oh, I say," purred Pearson. "I do like this one, Monty. Keep him close."

"Yes," said Rodin, his eyes only for Monty. "Keep me close."

Monty had no response. He looked around at his table of friends and marveled at how changeable their moods were. Every time he was on the verge of some sort of answer, the breeze blew and they were off on another tangent. It was beginning to quite annoy him.

"There's been no sign of the Weaver," Pearson said sometime later, his enunciation softened by the many glasses they'd all enjoyed. "I don't suppose you will see him tonight. He doesn't usually venture out this late."

"It can't be as late as all that, can it?" replied Bishop, but, in truth, he was only half paying attention to anything Pearson said. As the night had worn on, he and Leggy had gotten closer and closer until Leggy might have been sitting in his lap. They didn't even look at anyone else at the table so lost were they in their own quiet conversation.

The sea of sound that had surrounded them all evening suddenly dropped.

"Why have they stopped playing music?" asked Rodin.

"The special act of the evening will begin soon," answered Pearson. "You recall the ham and olives and such."

"The ham and olives will be singing?" asked Bishop with a laugh.

"Why don't we sing until the act begins?" suggested Leggy. "It's been ages since you and I sang together. Over three years, in fact. I remember when last we did, I was so nervous because you had proven yourself such a success—"

"I don't sing anymore," Bishop said sharply.

Leggy blinked in surprise. "But why ever not? It was the thing you used to love most."

"Please don't let's talk about that now. We have had such a lovely evening thus far."

Monty shook his head. Again, more mysteries that hovered just around the edge of things. It piqued him, and he found himself feeling at the end of his tether.

"Bishop." His voice was steely, causing everyone's attention to turn to him. "I must know why exactly we are searching for Weaver. At first I thought it was simply to gain access to the wonders of our friend here. But obviously there is more to it."

Bishop glanced at Leggy and Pearson. "Monty, maybe you ought to watch what you say."

"Come, Leggy," said Pearson. "I need to find the water closet. Help me."

"But it's just over there," said Leggy, baffled.

"Come, Leggy!" insisted Pearson. "And leave the fellows to their discussion."

"Oh, yes, sorry." Leggy jumped up and followed.

Monty measured his words.

"Monty, you shouldn't upset yourself," said Rodin, touching his arm.

Monty shrugged it off.

"No, I'm tired of being left in the dark. What is this all about, Bishop? And why does it all seem to be coming back to Paris? A subject, I might add, which makes you very much not yourself whenever it is raised."

"I shouldn't think you had very pleasant memories of Paris, either," snapped Bishop.

"It's true. For the most part, I don't. But it's over now, and times have changed."

Bishop gave him a caustic look. His voice, when he spoke, was bitter.

"Some things haven't changed in the slightest. Some things might just go on forever."

"Like what things? What is it you can't tell me?"

Bishop's eyes were a cloud of mystery. "Weaver helped me once before. He gave me advice and... instruction. For protection. I thought he might provide me with more."

"Protection? Against Rodin?"

Bishop laughed then, a rather caustic laugh but a laugh nonetheless.

"Oh, heavens, no, Monty. Our friend here seems totally innocuous. His brawn and beauty aside, he seems quite sweet, actually. I admit at first he confused me and the timing, well, the timing... But, no, I don't think I need protection from him."

"Then what?"

"Let's just forget about Weaver. Please, Monty. I am sorry, truly I am. I have caused you much hurt and annoyance, I see that now. But please trust me when I say there are some things, I simply cannot share."

Bishop met his gaze, and, in his eyes, Monty saw a deep pain he had never before noticed, the well of something unacknowledged and untenable. He wished he knew how he could help his friend.

"Well, if you insist..."

"I do, entirely."

Rodin put his hand on Monty's forearm and began to caress it. This time Monty did not fight him, but leaned into the touch, let it soothe him. He looked at Rodin. In those eyes he saw a tenderness that touched him. He saw comfort and, dare he think it, affection.

Rodin lifted Monty's hand to his mouth and kissed his fingers. In a night of confusion and anger, it felt like the one right thing. Just this, in this moment. Why had he been fighting this feeling since it had emerged? Monty had feared it would wash him out to sea if he gave in to it, but for now it felt like an anchor, the only solid thing holding him in place.

He smiled and Rodin smiled back.

"Did we miss the floor show?" asked a returned Leggy, glancing towards the stage.

"Which one?" asked Pearson.

"Do you know, Pearson, if you weren't so drunk, I would smack you across the mouth," said Bishop playfully.

"I've felt more threatened in a milliner's shop, dear Bishop."

The sound of guitars from the stage, more than one being strummed together, began to fill the room. A trio of voices, beautiful and somber, followed.

Rodin let out a small gasp. "*Un cante jondo*. I love this."

He turned around in his seat to gaze at the stage, and Monty, moved by his enthusiasm, did the same. The trio of men on the stage sang a haunting melody in Spanish, two of the men played guitars while the third added occasional flourishes with his accordion.

"*Gitanos*, from Spain," explained Pearson as the whole table studied the stage. "Mrs. Frye is nothing if not catholic in her taste."

"I always thought Mrs. Frye was Jewish?" said Leggy.

Pearson gave him a blank look. "Oh, Bishop. Capture this one quick before he melts in the rain."

"It is beautiful, is it not?" asked Rodin.

"Quite," agreed Monty.

The slow song began to pick up pace after a couple of minutes and the accordion player became more involved. The sound of a tambourine was heard offstage and then suddenly two women appeared. They both wore dresses of vivid patterns, with scarves wrapped around their heads. The one in the forefront, with no tambourine, unfurled a large, sheer scarf behind that fell almost to her ankles. While the other woman beat the rhythm on the tambourine and the men started to play with a certain clip and syncopation, the woman with the scarf held up began to dance and twirl about, moving her hips to the thumps of the tambourine, with her large, full sleeves also billowing like a cape.

Rodin stood and began to clap along with the song and move his hips similarly. He reached down and grabbed Monty's hand, pulling him up out of his seat.

"Move with me," he insisted. "You cannot sit for the flamenco."

Monty, perhaps a little too bright with alcohol, began to join in, laughing. He was no match for Rodin's moves but he clapped and swayed as the group sang and played.

"More like this," Rodin said, grabbing his hips and moving first to one side and then the other. Monty blushed and felt giddy, but he let the feeling overtake him, so exciting was the feel of Rodin's hands on his body.

"This Rodin fellow seems like a tonic," commented Pearson exhaling of his smoke.

"Or maybe something like tonic water," added Bishop.

"Do you know, my uncle swore tonic water was quite the curative," said Leggy. "He told me that all the soldiers would drink it when they were out in the deserts and all that. He was in the army, of course, for years and he still took it after. Mixed with a little gin."

"And he lived forever, pickled and smelling of juniper berries?" said Pearson.

"Actually, no. He died of malaria whilst on safari with one of his old army buddies. But I believe they almost shot quite a magnificent lioness."

Bishop laughed. "Oh, Leggy, you are a treasure." He leaned over his friend. "Here, Pearson, give us a cigarette, darling."

"It's my last one," Pearson protested. "You've smoked all the rest, you bastard."

"Only looking out for you, darling. Vile habit, smoking, I've always thought."

People all around the club were joining in with the clapping and Monty swayed to the music even more. He let his head roll on his shoulders as he gazed about the place, taking in the heady scene. Something caught his eye across the cavernous place and he came to a stop in dancing. The sight was like a splash of cold water in the face.

Rodin noticed and leaned into him. "What is wrong?"

Monty stood silently for a moment, trying to trace what he thought he'd seen as it moved through the shadows of the club. Rodin followed his gaze.

"Who do you see?" he asked.

Monty shook his head, blinking. "Nobody. I think. Too much wine, I'm afraid. It's gone to my head."

It couldn't be, he told himself. *How? Why would Friedrich be here? In this place, on this night?* It was too removed a chance to be real.

Rodin took Monty by the hips and kissed him deeply.

"Does that help to clear your head?" he asked.

Monty felt as if he might swoon. "Not especially, no. But at least the haze is more enjoyable now."

They turned back to their seats just as a new carafe of wine arrived.

"None for me, thank you," said Monty.

Pearson, Leggy, and Bishop weren't too shy to fill their glasses again.

Bishop took a gulp of wine and a puff on the cigarette. Bishop studied Rodin for a long moment, watching as he made sure Monty was feeling better.

Something caught Monty's eye, over Pearson's shoulder. It was the same form he saw earlier, only this time it was not mere shadows and slivers of light falling on features. He could see clearly that it was Friedrich, stalking along the walls of the club. He looked in their direction now, and Monty met his gaze.

All other noise fell away as Monty watched the nefarious form creep around.

It had to be him, there could be no mistaking it. Though it had been years now since he'd last seen him, he would remember those cruel eyes, that hard face. Friedrich stared at him, his lip curling up in a snarl. No, thought Monty, not again. He wasn't sure how this foul man had found them out once more, but he would not let him ruin their evening, nor bring his friend Bishop back into the cloud of anxiety which had hung around him in France.

"It's a rum business," Bishop was saying to Pearson. "Monty, don't you agree about this whole friendship my aunt has with that American? Quite a queer thing, no?"

Monty watched Friedrich, who snarled at him, and then turned away, stalking off.

"Hello, Monty?" Bishop snapped his fingers. "Are you quite awake?"

"Ah yes," said Monty distractedly. "Quite queer." He rose. "I'll be right back."

"Where the hell are you going?" asked Bishop.

"I'll get those cigarettes for you, Pearson. They sell them at the bar as I recall."

He began to move off, and felt someone grab his hand. It was Rodin.

"Everything is okay?"

"Don't worry. Yes, I'm fine." Rodin looked unconvinced. "You needn't worry. Shan't be a tick, you know."

Monty headed in the same direction as he had seen Friedrich go. He tried not to move too quickly as to seem odd and raise suspicion, but part of him wanted to run. To chase this awful man down, and pounce on him.

But as he followed the path Friedrich must have taken, he did not encounter him. He slipped through the people in the club and moved along the back wall, until he came to an end, a blank piece of wall with no exit. He peered around then, trying to see if he could place him. He saw no evidence of him, but he thought he might try the other side of the club, where he had seen him in the distance behind the *gitanos* performing. Monty moved swiftly, following the line of the bar, and then dashed to the wall behind the stage. He slunk along the wall, all the while tossing glances out over the tables of people, searching for the hulking figure.

But to no avail. He refused to believe it was all in his mind; he knew what he had seen. But if confrontation was not to be had, then he must get back to his friends. No matter what Bishop's plans for finding Weaver, he would convince his friends to leave. The night had gone on long enough.

He was shocked when he returned to the table and found only Pearson.

"Oh, Monty," he said, his drunken state all the more evident. "Where did you go? You forgot the cigarettes, I see."

"Where is everybody?"

"In the back, I believe."

"In the backrooms?" asked Monty, shocked. "But why on earth?"

"Well, I think they all followed that Freddy person."

"Freddy? Do you mean Uncle Freddy?"

Monty's pulse beat hard, anxiety poured through him.

"Yes. Some gentleman Bishop referred to as Freddy stopped by the table just after you left. Quite a rude fellow, I must say." Pearson hiccupped. "Oh, pardon me. At any rate, Bishop did not appear happy to see him, nor your French friend. He seemed to puff up when he saw this Freddy fellow, and they exchanged gazes of pure malice. But then this Freddy demanded to speak to Bishop in private. Rodin told him not to, but Bishop assured us all that it was all right. So off he went."

"With Freddy? To the backrooms?"

"Yes, that's right. But your friend was after them like a shot as soon as he saw them disappear behind the draperies. Oh, and before he left he said to me, "Tell Monty, I will make sure no harm comes to Bishop." Which perplexed me a little as it's only the backrooms, and the harm done there is usually consensual. Well, of course, dear Leggy didn't like the sound of that one bit, so he, too, was up and dashing after Rodin. And here I suddenly found myself alone and thought I ought to wait for you."

Monty began to move off.

"You're leaving then too?" Pearson said.

"I must. This Freddy person means no good will. I have to see if Bishop and Rodin are safe."

"Darling, it can't be dramatic as all that, can it?" Pearson stood up. "Shall I help?"

"I'm not sure what there is to do, but possibly you can help. Please find Mrs. Frye and let her know that there may be some shady goings on in the backrooms."

"Oh, Monty, I do think she's aware of that."

"No, something out of the ordinary. Something possibly dangerous."

"Good lord." Pearson suddenly seemed to sober up. "Yes, fine then. I will find her. Do be careful, Monty."

Monty turned again.

"You know, I am impressed at your zeal. You cut quite the hero, Monty, and it suits you. I hope you and this Rodin fellow continue. For someone you may or may not have met in Paris and then may or may not have been discovered in a lake somehow, the two of you certainly make a fine pairing."

Monty nodded his thanks and moved quickly off.

Chapter Eleven

One might call the Back Rooms regally appointed if one were so inclined, although the last royal to indulge in such excessive luxury was likely the Prince Regent. On plush couches and lounges all around men draped themselves, overcome by any number of urges. Too much drink, too much opium, too much carnal knowledge needed of any man who passed through the draperies. Compared to what lay beyond in the area called The Caverns, these rooms were tame, but the atmosphere was obvious all the same. Male bodies, of all shapes and sort, in various stages of undress, lazed about here. Some interlocked with other bodies, some prowling the perimeters of the space.

Although the backrooms offered a small world of delights, they had been known to house tricksters and thieves, a thought which only heightened Monty's anxiety. Men intent on either robbing you or amassing enough incriminating evidence to continue robbing you in secret outside. Blackmail it was called when anyone had the nerve to utter the word, and no one ever did. Monty had never been one to go past the draperies and investigate these clandestine spaces but he knew that Bishop had frequented them many times over the few years the Brunswick had been in operation. Bishop came to escape—to lose himself in carnal desire and to mentally obliterate his ties to the real world. To forget the judgment of society, to forget his place and his obligations, to not be, even for one brief moment, the man the world forced him to be. Monty only hoped that, in following Friedrich back here, Bishop had not found himself obliterated entirely.

A cherubic young man jogged by, wearing no clothing but holding a serving tray. Monty assumed him to be staff, and, judging by the red splotches of heat, which colored not only his cheeks but his arse as well, he assumed him to be knowledgeable of what was going on in the back. Monty put out a hand to stop him.

"Yes, sir, how can I serve you?" the young man asked, batting his thick eyelashes.

"No need for any of that, my dear boy," Monty said kindly. "I am trying to find my friends."

Monty described the departed trio.

"I'm sure I'd have noticed a group of that description, sir. But I haven't seen them. Definitely not up here, anyway." He gave a coy smile. "You might try the Caverns though; seems more the space for them."

Monty steeled his nerve and headed towards the entrance into the Caverns. It was a long hallway, darker here and rougher, as the formal structure of the legal entity of the club ended at the Back Rooms. Here began a series of warrens carved from the underground rock and were said, by some, to be from the ancient parts of the city, before civilization even. The stone walls were rough at points and smooth at others, with large juts and slabs sticking out in certain spaces. They made Monty think of Druid altars and pagan rituals, and while the association might have been mysterious and thrilling at any other time, now it only felt ominous. The electric lighting of the backrooms ended at this point as well, part secrecy, part practicality, and the way was lit at first by gas sconces and then deeper by torches of raw flame.

Noises echoed against these dungeon-lined walls as well. Primal and disturbing, at least to someone with Monty's sensibilities. The moans and soft groans of the backrooms turned into pleading, barks of command and shouts of passion, as well as the occasional crack of a whip, along with low, animal-like sounds. Men, obscured by the shadows, leaned against the ragged stone walls, their hungry looks washing over anyone who passed, seeking invitations to be given or taken. Others still were huddled around, panting in great packs, erect and stroking as they watched acts in progress; partners in all manner of coitus; individuals stroking or displaying for the enjoyment of others, giving them a show.

Monty always felt a slight aversion to such libertinage, preferring the intimacy of one partner. But, at the moment, he was too concerned to even register the activities surrounding him. Suddenly strong hands grabbed him and pulled him sideways, off his path, and he found himself tumbling into the solid body of a giant man. The bounder had to be at least six foot six and he was stripped to the waist, his great barrel chest exposed and glowing with perspiration. For a moment panic flared, as he thought Friedrich might be accosting him, determined to halt his investigating.

Monty threw up his hands to steady himself, and felt the hairy muscled torso beneath them. He looked up at the rugged face; the man was dark but had blue eyes that glinted in the gaslight. He felt relieved that it was not Friedrich. The stranger put a large hand under Monty's chin and jerked his head up, trying to pull him into a kiss. Monty pushed him away.

"No need to be coy. I know what you want," whispered the man hotly.

"I'm afraid not. Just now I'm looking for a friend."

The man chuckled, low and gruff.

"Ain't we all, guv. Ain't we all."

Monty pushed away from him and started back on his path; the man grabbed his arm.

"If you don't find your particular friend, guv; you'll remember where I am. I can be your friend, too."

Monty jerked his arm away and moved off. Far down, where this corridor ended, there seemed to be a great stream of light pouring into the edge of the darkness. It appeared to be some sort of larger room, and Monty picked up his pace to reach it.

He came to the end of the stony hallway and virtually stumbled into the space there, the light beaming from inside so bright he had to hold his arm up to shield his eyes. Stepping into the room the air was thick and it felt as if crossing through some invisible barrier of some sort. Like breaking surface tension and falling into a body of water. He found himself in a large high-ceilinged cave. Torches fastened to the wall by way of sconces embedded in the stone illuminated the space. There were many torches but still not enough to explain the heat of the space, especially this far into the underground. The air seemed to shimmer from the heat, as it did in the desert above the sand.

Monty was in a swollen crowd of men who all faced one direction in the cavern. The throng were in various stages of undress, some stripped to the waist, some only in their underclothes, some completely naked. Their skin all glistened from sweat and they seemed to breathe as one, their chests moving in and out, their stomachs clenching at the same pace. Some were slack-jawed, others with their lips sealed, but they all had a glassy look in their eyes. They stared up and ahead, as if transfixed, as if mesmerized. Those with their mouths closed hummed in unison, those with their mouths open seemed to moan; together they made a sound like the roar of a coal engine, the feel of the sound mimicking the shimmering air around them. It was a bizarre and unsettling sight to Monty. As if they had all become mindless creatures, captivated by some spell.

The light here was as different as the air, and it was clear this was not a normal state. It pulsed and moved, crashing against the walls and creating a haze, like the foamy mist of a crashing wave. The heat and the light palpitated, like a heartbeat, a moving force that could not be seen but was felt. The Caverns were known among those who knew of them as a hedonistic, secretive—sometimes even debauched—part of the club which eschewed the rules of the rest of the space.

But this was not ordinary. There was a presence here that felt like evil, like a tangible darkness that slithered over the bodies of all assembled here.

The heat closed in on him as he tried to push his way through the crowd, and he began to struggle to breathe. His labored breathing turned into a great rumbling in his chest, and he was compelled to join in with the humming crowd around him. But a force inside him rejected it, and he closed his eyes, concentrating, and was somehow able to dispel the urge. He found himself thinking of Rodin, and in his mind's eye he zeroed in on the warm glowing image of the man. Monty felt as if he were absorbing the golden glow of Rodin's skin and that glow suffused him, cooling him down and focusing his mind so that the haze dissipated.

Opening his eyes, he found himself nearer the front of the crowd and he could finally see clearly. He followed the line of catatonic stares of those around him and saw before him what appeared to be an altar.

Monty gasped. His skin crawled at what he saw.

Freidrich was there, stripped to the waist, his chest and arms and shoulders swollen with muscle, almost thrice his normal size. He appeared taller, bigger, and broader than Monty had ever seen him. His trousers strained against the muscles of his lower body, his feet were bare where they had burst through his socks and shoes. His body was covered in patches of something like fur—its texture seemed to exist somewhere between a wolf pelt and the shiny, coarse covering of a sea lion—and new growths of it seemed to spring up, covering his skin, even as Monty studied him. His head was now elongated, like the muzzle of a hyena or a jackal, and on the sides of his head, his ears had grown long and pointed, standing like small horns.

A naked man lay a few feet ahead of him, discarded on the floor, a wound in his neck. The wound was fresh, but it was ragged, torn, as if he had been bitten by some great animal. In his hand, the man still clutched a thin shard of stone, tapered, almost like a small word or a dagger, its end stained with fresh blood. Monty stared, trying to discern if the man was dead or alive, until he saw the man cough, a small splatter of blood dancing across his lips. The man turned on his side moaning, and Monty saw his face.

"My god!" he exclaimed.

The man hovering on the edge of life, his throat ripped open, was Leggy. Monty rushed forward. He tried to lift Leggy's head, tapping his cheeks, but Leggy was not responsive. His eyes rolled back in his head, and he breathed with a sputtering sound. The wound on his neck began to emit more blood and Monty, frightened, laid him back on the floor, not knowing what to do.

He looked up at the monstrous Friedrich. It was only then that he realized that the man Friedrich was holding, lankly sprawled on one arm, was Bishop. A great pain pierced Monty's chest. Bishop's head lolled to one side and although his eyes were open he did not seem conscious. They were glassy and blank with a lack of life. Like the men who stood around watching this spectacle, he had somehow been mesmerized, except into an even deeper state, and his body hung as if lifeless. His shirt had been ripped open, exposing the flesh of his torso, and it glowed pale and bright in the light of the torches.

Monty stormed forward.

"You bastard!" he cried.

"STOP!"

Friedrich's voice shattered the room like a crack of thunder. His eyes were like bursts of flame. His face shifted and morphed, looking at once animal and only slightly human.

"Come no further!" he commanded. His voice sounded like a chorus of voices, all speaking as one.

Monty took a few more steps forward, unheeding and Friedrich held up his hand. Some invisible force knocked Monty back and he stumbled, almost falling.

"Unhand my friend," he yelled.

Friedrich waved dismissively and again some force hit Monty, knocking him, this time, to the floor.

"This," stormed Friedrich, "is none of your concern, boy. You were always too meddlesome. And I shall have done with you soon."

"What are you doing?" demanded Monty. "What is all this?"

"Something you do not understand, human," answered Friedrich.

Human? The word flashed through Monty's mind.

"You're damned right," he shouted. "I do not understand this madness. You will release my friend this instant!"

Friedrich began to laugh, a noise like a grinding stone, a many-voiced laugh, human, animal, a consort of sounds, all at once, as if more than one creature resided within him.

He held up the hand with which he had repelled Monty. The hand began to shift, change form, the skin growing darker, its surface tough and lined, rough like the hide of a skinned animal. His fingernails grew into threatening, dangerous claws, pointed at the end, razor-sharp. Monty's mind flashed for a second to earlier that night, watching Rodin's transformation, but this was something much more gruesome and stomach-churning.

Friedrich ran one pointed claw from underneath Bishop's ear down his chest, his smooth, hairless skin glowing gold. The claw did not pierce the skin, but it appeared dangerously close.

"No!" cried Monty, jumping up and trying to charge. "What gives you the right to do this?"

"This boy, this human, this friend of yours," said Friedrich, his voice crunchy and hoarse, "he owes me a debt. Long unpaid!"

He ran the long nail of his claw back up Bishop's chest and came to a stop at his throat.

"A debt of blood!" he roared.

He flicked his hand then and a thin but long line of scarlet appeared on Bishop's neck.

"You monster!" screamed Monty. "What are you doing?"

"Silence!" demanded Friedrich, his hand in the air again, he closed it in a tight fist.

Monty gulped and suddenly began to feel as if he were choking. He grabbed at his neck and he felt the air being twisted out of it.

"You will keep your mouth shut, human!" cried Friedrich. "Or yours shall be the next throat I rip out."

He unclenched his fist, splaying his fingers, and Monty threw back his head gasping. He felt the air rush into his throat again and he choked on it. The air and heat rushed in around, like it had before, and was overcome by it. Monty could not fight it off in the moment and his body gave way. Falling to his knees, coughing and sputtering, he shook his head, trying to clear the turbid feeling—his mind muddy, unclear.

He looked up from his fallen spot and watched as Freidrich tossed Bishop from one arm to the other. Bishop's head rolled so that he faced Monty directly now. His eyes empty, his mouth frozen in a gasp. Monty saw his friend there, sprawled like a corpse, a trickle of blood from the earlier wound seeping down his shoulder and staining the shirt that still clung there.

Monty's eyes welled with tears. He felt helpless, trapped.

Freidrich had raised his free hand, also transformed, and his claw glinted in the light. He threw his head back, and his mouth was like the jaw of a wolf or a bear, wide and full of teeth like knife blades. He roared then, his eyes fixed on Bishop's flesh.

"No, please," Monty said, but his voice was little more than a ragged, pitiful whisper.

He closed his eyes against the horror, trying to summon up the will to overcome the evil weight pressing on his body and mind. Again, he conjured the image of Rodin, glowing, strong, full of light. The picture of Rodin grew and grew in his mind, swelling so that it totally overcame anything else he sensed. He felt himself flooded with the light and the power of his imagining until, even with his eyes closed, he saw a powerful flooding of golden light that overtook all else. He heard a loud snap, a break like a clap of thunder and then all went black.

He blinked open his eyes, distraught. "Rodin," he whispered. "Rodin, please."

He cringed as Friedrich roared again, even louder than before, his head moving as if to attack. Monty tried to stand, his footing unsteady and weak. He stumbled and fell again. There was a loud sound like a pack of wild dogs all howling at once. A shot of light moved through the atmosphere, like the reverberation of a shotgun. There was a blur of movement; a body leaping from the crowd and pouncing on Friedrich's back.

Friedrich roared and threw back his arm trying to claw the body off him, but to no avail. Monty saw

that the body which had leapt on him was that of
Rodin. He too had been stripped to the waist and
wounds marred his flesh as well. Long lines that had
been cut in, presumably by a set of claws, but which
seemed to be healing. Around his waist was wound
a length of chain, which he had tied like a belt at the
front. On his ankles were matching shorter lengths
of chain that had been broken, snapped free of a
constraint of some sort. An image flashed in Monty's
mind. The chains around Rodin's waist were the
same coppery green metal of the bracelet which
Friedrich had always worn in Paris. The bracelet that
looked like a small link chain with the circled dot
symbol of alchemy at its center.

Rodin wrapped his arms around Friedrich's
swollen neck, pulling back and twisting his head.
Friedrich, now completely transformed into a massive creature like a demonic black wolf or dog standing on its hindquarters, roared in anger. The sound
shook the room and Monty winced, expecting at any
moment stones to fall from the ceiling. Friedrich
threw his free hand behind him, over his shoulder, his claws flexing and shredding the air. His
arm flailed and his claws found their target, slicing
through the exposed flesh of Rodin's back.

Rodin cried out in pain, and Monty cried out
as well, his heart wracked with worry. Despite his
wounds, Rodin did not relent. He wrapped one arm
around the beast's throat, anchoring himself, and
then he punched into Friedrich's shoulder with all
his might. Friedrich cried out in rage and pain and
he dropped Bishop's body onto the stone floor.

Rodin struck again and Friedrich fell back, trying to throw himself against the ragged walls to rid himself of Rodin.

Monty took his chance and rushed forward to his fallen friend's side.

"Bishop, Bishop," he cried, "Can you hear me?"

He got no response so he slipped his hands under Bishop's arms, dragging him away. He scampered back with all his might, trying to get his friend as much distance as he could away from the fray. The movement caught Friedrich's eye, even as he fought, and he howled in anger. With a flourish of supreme fury, he swelled with power. He reached around, grabbing Rodin by the throat and tossed him, like a small pup, flinging him against the wall. Rodin smashed into the rock surface with a grunt of pain and crumpled to the floor. Friedrich eyed Monty and began to rush towards him. For so large and hulking a creature, he moved with incredible speed, and Monty knew there was nothing he could do to avoid his onslaught.

"Give me what belongs to me!" roared Friedrich in that warped voice, which sounded like the cacophonous crush of a thousand suffering souls.

Monty felt himself scream as the beast ran towards him, but then another sound even louder than his own bellow overtook the atmosphere. It was Rodin, recovered and chasing Friedrich. He loosened the length of chain wound around his waist, and it began to glow under his touch. The glow spread over his form and he beamed with otherworldly light in the same way Monty had imagined him behind closed eyes. With a howling bark, Rodin jumped, leaping through the air and once again landed on Friedrich's back. This time, however, he wrapped the glowing chain around that great hairy neck and brought him up short. Rodin howled again, his fierce bark of anger, and tightened the chain, his muscles flexing to their full. The chain glowed brighter than before, shooting of rays of light, like the flames of a wild fire, and began to sear into Friedrich's flesh. With another yank, full of all the force he had within his form, Rodin twisted the glowing chain. There was a loud cracking noise, like the sound of hot water shattering a cold glass, but many decibels louder.

The noise in Friedrich's throat went silent and he stumbled forward. The chain around his neck flared blue-bright hot and Rodin released it, jumping off the creature's back. Friedrich's body was a sudden tangle of limbs, all control over itself lost, and he fell, muzzle first, smashing into the ground.

The chain flared even brighter and burst into flames, flames which consumed Friedrich's entire form. His body burned, exploding into a large engulfing flame, and in seconds, he was gone, completely. Not even ash remained, only a shallow, thin pool of silvery blue liquid, oily and reflective, that quivered in the space where he had gone down.

The temperature of the room dropped immediately, the glassy-eyed men who had stood around, humming the whole time, came to. The room suddenly silent, they all gazed around, blinking and befuddled.

Monty heard a gasp of air and saw his friend blinking back into consciousness.

"Bishop, Bishop, are you all right?"

"Monty? What is happening Monty?"

Bishop tried to sit up and let out a yelp of pain; his
hand flew to the wound in his neck.

"No, not yet," said Monty. "Give yourself some
time."

"Oh my god, Monty. Leggy!"

They both looked up and saw Rodin, bleeding and
bruised, carrying Leggy's naked body. He placed
Leggy down by the pool of liquid that Friedrich's
body had left behind. Rodin dipped his hands into
the pool of liquid and moved them over Leggy.
Monty was confused and repelled but didn't dare
call out; somehow he felt sure Rodin knew what
he was doing. Rodin let the liquid pour into the
ragged wound on Leggy's throat and then smeared
it onto his skin, touching all the places that had been
hurt. The cloying silverish liquid was absorbed and
Monty and Bishop both gasped as they watched the
wound close up and appear healed, as if by magically. Rodin then put his hands back into the unctuous
substance and coated them. He then slowly rubbed
his hands all over Leggy's entire body, the liquid
shimmering under his touch, and then sat back on
his haunches, waiting.

There was a deep, long gasp as Leggy threw back
his head and began to suck in air. He turned his
head, coughing repeatedly, until all the blood had
been expelled. He sat up then, dazed and wiping his
mouth against the back of his arm.

"What? W-w-where am I?" Leggy stuttered.

"You are all right now," Rodin assured him.

Rodin looked around, calling out, "Does anyone have any water?"

One of the men who had been transfixed ran forward with a bottle of wine.

"This will have to do," Rodin said. He pressed the bottle into Leggy's hand. "Drink. You must repair your throat."

Leggy nodded, taking a gulp. He winced in pain but shook it off and kept gulping. Meanwhile, Rodin went once more to the pool of liquid and cupped his hands in it. He began walking to where Monty and Bishop were still crouched on the floor.

Bishop began pushing his feet against the stone floor, pressing Monty back.

"No, no," he cried. "I am not so wounded. I know that comes from him! I want no part of that man—that creature—on me ever again."

Monty stroked his hair and tried to steady him.

"Bishop, you must. It may be the only way to heal such a wound."

Rodin got closer and Bishop wriggled and thrashed, but as Rodin kneeled over him and let the liquid fall onto his skin, he settled. Rodin traced a line along the cuts on his chest and then up to his throat. The wounds and the skin healed within seconds and Monty felt Bishop relax, finally, in his arms.

His eyes were closed and he breathed deeply, and Monty knew he must be exhausted beyond knowing. From this night, from the fear he had been carrying for so long, the knowledge of this creature and its deadly nature.

Monty looked up at Rodin.

"How do you know about all of this? How to heal? How to destroy that—that thing?"

"My history is long. I have encountered much in my time."

Monty wanted to know more, but he imagined there was not time enough in the world to know all that Rodin had seen. Still, maybe he would. Someday. For now, he was content enough in the knowledge that his friend was safe, and the danger destroyed.

Monty helped Bishop get to his feet and began to button up his blood-stained shirt. Rodin sorted through the piles of clothing that had been hurled into the back of the cave unwittingly by the hexed men, who now searched for their belongings, and found something for Leggy to wear.

"Good god in Christ!"

Monty heard the familiar voice and saw Pearson standing at the entrance of the cave, holding multiple coats and hats over his arms, gaping at the scene he found.

"What in the world has happened here?" he exclaimed.

"Far too much to explain," said Monty with a heavy voice.

"I should think so," agreed Pearson. "We heard strange and horrific sounds as far in as the bar just now."

"Will the police be summoned?"

"Probably have already been by somebody," said Pearson. "But not by Mrs. Frye. She had some feeling the chaos that could be heard had to do with you lot so she sent me with your coats and things. She harbors no ill will, she explained but she doesn't need or want to know what has occurred. Only that it is over and she has no knowledge of it to either confirm or deny." He pointed to one side of the great stone dais that had served as the altar space for Friedrich's heinous act. "Also, she says, there is an exit just behind there which take you out of the building and back onto the streets. She prefers you use that and not come back through the club."

"Thank you," said Monty, taking the clothing from him. "Are you coming with us?"

Pearson shook his head. "I promised I would let Mrs. Frye know that all was secured and that there weren't any major ...damages to account for." Pearson peered around at the mass of half-naked men wandering around and dressing themselves. His eyes lingered on the pools of liquid that were slowly evaporating. "And as things don't look entirely different from the end of a night in the Caverns, I shall report as such. Then I shall exit quickly by the front entrance. I've yet to be caught in a raid, and I have no plans to begin a new trend." He paused. "That is, if everything is as well as can be?"

"Everyone is alive, though possibly confused and some a little battered. But they should be fine once they get some fresh night air into them. I hope."

"Then I shall call on you all tomorrow, or the next day, to check in when you've sufficient time to recover. That is, unless someone is in need of a place to stay? I am still in the rooms I shared with Jonas until the end of the month if anyone needs."

"No need, old chap," said a beleaguered Bishop. "Plenty of room for everyone at the townhouse."

"Right. I'm off then. I would suggest you make haste as well; Mrs. Frye informs me the tunnel to the street is not short." He looked at Bishop. "And if I see the Weaver chap, I'll let him know you're looking for him, shall I?"

Bishop shook his head.

"I doubt there's a need for that now, old chap."

Pearson nodded, cast one more studied glance around the space, and trotted back to the front of the establishment.

Leggy came up to Bishop just then, having clothed himself and threw his arms around the man.

"I thought you might have died," he said, tears choking his words.

Bishop patted him on the back and then pulled him closer.

"I thought the same of you, my dear boy. And weren't you something like a hero rushing back here like that. My heart nearly burst when I saw you raging forth like that against that bastard creature. Sword in hand like some storybook prince."

Leggy sniffed and raised his head. "It was foolish, I know. Once I got back here and saw that he had somehow restrained Rodin—twice my size—in those chains, I knew there was no point to trying."

"And yet you did."

"It was stupid, I know."

Bishop stared deep into his eyes. "You are a stupid, wonderful, brave, brave boy."

Leggy nodded. Bishop took his face in his hands and kissed him deeply but sweetly. Leggy fell against his chest and buried his face in the torn and stained shirt.

Monty looked over at Rodin. He had found shoes but was still naked from the waist up. His skin glowed in the light, as perfect as the moment Monty first saw him by the lake, all the cuts and scrapes and perforations now gone, healed and invisible.

"Friedrich managed to restrain you?" asked Monty, finding it hard to believe after the show of power and agility he had shown earlier.

"Only after he got those chains wrapped around him," said Bishop. "What the devil were those anyway?"

"Chains of Atlantean Orichalcum," said Rodin. "The strongest substance known. Almost as ancient as him. I might normally have been able to them loose with little effort but he had enchanted them as well, somehow. They drained me as soon as he wrapped them around me; I had no strength."

"Then how did you manage to break them?" asked Monty.

"I used their power to tap into my own," explained Rodin. "I closed my eyes and imagined myself. I tapped into the most powerful emotions I had and I could see myself glowing, radiating light, and I felt the chains absorb that light. Then suddenly I had control and they became malleable in my hands. I snapped them in two and wound them about my waist to use them."

"And when you knew what Friedrich's intentions were with Bishop, you were able to summon these depths of anger to focus your power?" Monty tried to clarify.

Rodin shook his head, looking slightly abashed.

"No. Anger was not my most powerful emotion. I thought of what the aufhocker's actions would do to Bishop, and how any harm that came to Bishop would wound you and break your heart. The thought of your pain and sorrow, I could not stand it. I found the power then. With those thoughts of you."

Monty was speechless; he stood staring at Rodin.

Rodin approached him and pulled him close. He kissed him. It was not a short kiss, and Monty's head began to swim. The cavern around them disappeared, the stench and the heat, the light of the torches, it all dissolved into a cool, darkness. Like treading water in the river on a hot summer day, he felt suspended and relieved. He ran his hands up and down Rodin's back, feeling the strong muscles and the smooth, smooth skin that had not long ago been scarred from battle. A battle that had been won by the power of affection for him, a power that he felt from Rodin, pushing and growing even in this moment.

Nearby, Bishop cleared his throat.

"Well," Bishop said dryly. "I suppose I should appreciate that I factored into Rodin's decision to defeat the beast, one way or another. But we might hasten to exit, before we're all faced to deal with the beast called law enforcement."

He put his hand on Monty's shoulder, shaking from his stupor.

"Come now, let's get this titan of yours dressed. As marvelous as he may be, he can't go out into the streets stripped to the waist. Not in this part of London, at least."

"The pile in the back seems to have been all taken away except for a few pieces," offered Leggy.

"I don't suppose anything would fit him anyway," said Bishop. "But Freddy did discard his jacket behind the altar, just before he began to.... to transform. It's only a jacket, but he's the only one anywhere near Rodin's build."

Monty grimaced. "Must we use his garments?"

"I think we must, Monty. Mrs. Frye did supply us with ample warning but the ampleness has grown thin."

The group of them moved behind the "altar" as Pearson had indicated and found an ancient-looking wooden door hinged into the rock face. Pulling it open they found a passageway. It was another corridor of sorts carved into the stone. Just feet before them, the floor slanted upwards, a seemingly steep climb into the pitch black. Monty shivered, altogether not in the mood for another secret passageway, and, too, trying not to let his mind think on the reasons such an escape route had once been created in this hidden away space of the Caverns. What long ago scenes had been played out in this underground world, and had they always been as maniacal as Friedrich's sacrifice. He hoped he would find no answers to his questions on their way to the surface.

Rodin came up beside them, having gone back into the space to retrieve a torch. He moved to the front of the group to lead them.

"Come along, chaps," Bishop encouraged. "The only way to get out is to move forward."

They stepped into the darkness, hoping he was right.

Chapter Twelve

Paris, 1907

It was still quite early in the morning, just past dawn, and the Latin Quarter was only beginning to awaken. Still, Monty stood there, just across the avenue which ran in front of the Panthéon, staring up at the statue he had visited so often.

He pulled his coat tight against the morning chill and exhaled, watching his breath billow like a cloud of smoke.

It had been three weeks since he had seen Bishop in the flesh. Bishop had not returned to their hotel the night after the incident with Freidrich in the opera house. Nor had he returned the next day or the next. A week went by before Monty had heard anything from his friend, a week frantic with worry. Finally he had received a letter, by way of the hotel, from Bishop explaining that he was all right and that he had gone back to Les Mans to spend some time alone. He assured Monty that their hotel bill was covered and he would not stay away, only that he needed a bit of fresh air to clear his mind.

The frantic worry had, in a way, been a welcome distraction. It had been three weeks, also, since Trevor had abandoned him by the fountain. He wasn't sure he would recover from that blow, or even, really, if he wanted to recover. Sometimes, he mused, it was easier to swaddle one's self in heartbreak and shut out the world. Keep the possibility for ever getting hurt again at bay; learn to be content in the total lack of love in your life, and explain away that lack as something that keeps you strong.

Yet Monty did not feel strong.

Perhaps Bishop had been right all along. Perhaps love was not a thing they could manage in this world. Perhaps it was something that would always be just out of reach.

For three weeks, he had wandered Paris utterly alone. For three weeks, he had woven a cape of solitude and wondered how it might fit him in days to come.

Leggy had shown up at the hotel once or twice, inquiring after Bishop. And they had suffered two or three forlorn lunches, neither of them wanting to speak about the sudden disappearance of love, neither of them wanting to talk of anything else. And so the lunches went by silently, until at last, thankfully, even Leggy stopped coming.

Three weeks of near silence without solace.

Until, finally, a letter had arrived from Bishop last week.

It had simply read,

"I am ready to go back home, friend. Aren't you? Next Monday."

And Monty agreed he was ready.

So here he was again, one last time, standing and looking at *The Thinker*. He did not know why this particular statue brought him such comfort but it did. It wasn't the artist's best work, and the idea, the subject, was truly, if one thought about it, rather insipid. Yet he was drawn to it time and time again. Only to stand and study its form, its curves, to be reminded of stability and force.

He glanced at his watch and saw that it was time to get back to the hotel.

He began to walk away but he felt the sensation that someone was watching him. He turned back in the direction of *The Thinker* and glanced about. He thought he saw a shadowy form move just underneath where the statue sat, but the Quarter was coming alive now with everyday life, so it could have been anybody or anything.

Maybe, he thought fantastically, it was *The Thinker* he felt staring at him. Watching him recede as he had watched it so many mornings.

Or, perhaps it was just a ghost of Paris.

Paris had many ghosts. And they threatened to haunt him for some time to come.

As he made the entrance to the hotel, the doors opened and out walked Bishop.

He wanted to run up and embrace his old friend. But, of course, propriety dissuaded that, and, too, so did Bishop's body language.

"All of our things are already packed in the cab," Bishop said by way of greeting.

"Bishop, are you all right? It's been so long. How have you been?"

Bishop was drawn, sickly. His luster was gone. Monty had never seen him so unlike himself. His voice was soft, his manner dour.

Bishop did not answer immediately. Instead he took time pulling on and fastening his gloves. Finally he met Monty's gaze, his expression a mask.

"Come, my dear friend, it's time we go home. Let's leave Paris behind us for good."

Chapter Thirteen

London, 1910

Outside, on the streets behind the Brunswick, the air had taken a slight chill from earlier in the evening. The two couples had stumbled up the last rocky steps of the caverns and pushed open the disguised door to find themselves in an alleyway near Regent Street. It was still quite dark and the street lamps were lit.

The four of them stood there, looking out in all directions, not really seeing anything, merely regaining their bearings. It was hard to believe that they had only just been beneath Regent Street, in all its ordinariness, when what had occurred seemed like a visitation from some alternate realm of reality. They were silent as they stretched their limbs, feeling the familiar air against their skin.

"It's awfully late," Leggy said finally.

"Or awfully early," said Monty. "I think we're closer now to dawn than dusk."

There was a slight hum and then Bishop sang,
And how her rosy fingers wove the clouds
Into a morn just like a shroud

Monty and Leggy stared at him gape-mouthed. His voice was rough, slightly strained, but still as lovely as it had been in his youth.

"My god, Bishop," said Monty. "I haven't heard you sing in three years."

Bishop studied the pavement for a moment. He brought his hand to his throat and rubbed it.

"But, of course, I couldn't, you see. Never singing, that was how I kept Friedrich at bay for so long. The Weaver helped me with that. So long as I didn't act on the gifts he had given, Freddy had no rights over me."

"All this time, you were denying your voice to keep him at bay?" asked Monty.

Bishop nodded. "Or at least, that's how it ought to have been. But creatures like Freddy will exact their price no matter what."

"Then the blood pact he spoke of, that was in payment?"

"For my voice, yes."

"But you could already sing," insisted Monty.

"Not like I did in Paris, Monty. You know that. When Freddy came to me, I had no idea who or what he was. A patron, I thought. An older man who, like so many before him, came to me with promises simply for my company. But then my voice began to change. It was astonishing. The depths and highs I had never had, the color and pliability. Singing felt all new, transcendent even. I couldn't believe what music had become for me.

"It was then that he asked me what I wanted most in my life. And I told him that I wanted to be able to captivate anybody and everybody with my voice. That I might use it to change minds, to bend wills, to bring whatever success or solace I needed. I wanted to be able to bring anybody I wanted most to my side, and keep them there."

Bishop looked at Leggy then.

"And it worked."

Leggy grabbed his hand. "Bishop, you did not need any gifts you didn't already have. You already had so many in abundance, and you already had so many willing to stand by your side."

"Not so many before," Bishop said. "But one, most assuredly, as I see now."

"But the aufhocker's gift came with a price," said Rodin.

"Yes," said Bishop. "A very dear price. He wanted my blood, my life force. And when I refused it, he became quite angry, violent. I managed to trick him long enough to leave Paris, but once we were back in England, I did not know what to do. So I sought out Weaver then and he gave me guidance. But, he promised me, it was not forever—nothing could keep the beast at bay indefinitely. One day, he would find me. And about three months ago, he did.

"I saw him out in public, in a social setting. He didn't make a scene when people were around, but I saw him on the edges, stalking me. And I ran. I ran home that night and gathered what I could and fled to my parents' estate."

"And within a few days, your apartment was empty and vacated."

"Yes, sorry about that, Monty. I knew that confused you. But, as you can see now, I couldn't explain. Not all of this."

"You could have confided in me," Monty said. "I would have understood."

"Would you have?" asked Bishop, his tone somber. "Look at how deeply you questioned your own wishes realized through the mystical."

Monty and Rodin exchanged a look, and Monty knew he could not argue that point.

"Bishop had no idea what Friedrich was really capable of," Rodin explained. The violence, the depravity, few could imagine really. Unless it was something you had seen before."

"I thought maybe your showing up was somehow connected, at first. Once I accepted that another mystical creature had somehow discovered me—us—I thought surely it must mean something."

"I am afraid I did not know of Friedrich's presence here before tonight," confessed Rodin. "I only came in search of Monty."

"Yes, I see that now," said Bishop. "But, whether you knew it or not, I think you also must have come for me. Because, otherwise, where would we all be at this moment? I'm grateful to you."

"And I am grateful too," said Leggy. "For this chance."

Rodin smiled at them both and turned to Monty.

"And you, Montgomery Singer. Are you also grateful for me?"

"Perhaps." A smile curved Monty's lips, but he narrowed his eyes as he replied, "But not if you call me Montgomery ever again."

Rodin laughed. "You tease me."

"Perhaps."

Bishop stumbled in his place, and leaned against a wall for support. Leggy rushed over to him.

"I think we shall hail a cab," Leggy said. "He's far too exhausted to walk."

"Yes, of course," said Monty. "Rodin and I shall walk. We have things to discuss."

There was a full moon as they walked, which thought Monty quite appropriate. It gave the city a certain shading in these late hours. The street lights cast hazy blooms of light as they competed with the moon, standing at attention and peering down on the streets like bleary-eyed Cyclopes. They watched over London, helping to keep it safe, yet they were a constant reminder that the night did not belong solely to the citizens. Only shadows were in need of illumination, and shadows held mystery and danger.

Monty was, for some reason, compelled to head for Hyde Park, and he led them in that direction. Rodin did not argue nor press him to talk; they both seemed content, for this little while, to walk silently and feel warmed by the safeness of one another's presence. It had been a very long night, and there was nothing yet to say.

As they walked they passed the south side of Grosvenor Square. Monty studied the snug houses facing the garden square, all, despite their minor cosmetic differences, so very much the same, and thought of his parents. Long asleep, to be sure, and cosseted by their sense of security and the surety of love. Would that ever be a surety he would know? As Bishop had so often reminded him, the world offered so very little in the way of guarantees for men like them. Would he ever know a forever, a love ensured?

"Before," Monty began. "You said you came here for me?"

"Yes," answered Rodin.

"But how is that possible?"

"We selkies can go very far, to many places, no matter the distance or time."

They had reached the outskirts of Hyde Park and it was quiet, but only softly so. Monty could hear the trees sway and, somewhere in the distance, he strained to hear what he thought was the gentle lap of the waves in the Serpentine Lake. He reckoned that they probably were not allowed to be in the park at such a time, but they hiked on, unheeding.

"Of course I have certainly been awakened to the breadth of your abilities this evening," said Monty with a smile as they strolled more. "But what I mean to say is, why did you come for *me*? How did you know who I am?"

"But I have known you since Paris."

"So you said. Our fates were somehow intertwined there?"

"Yes."

"But can you tell me how?"

"I saw you first, when you came to the Seine. You would come to it in many places throughout the city, standing at its edges, looking out over it. I was captivated by you and I began to seek you out."

"For the entirety of my time in France?"

"So, in essence, you stalked me just as Friedrich stalked Bishop?"

Rodin halted suddenly, looking at him intently. "Please do not make such a comparison. It hurts me. I did not stalk you like that creature. Merely I watched you, kept an eye on you, and ensured that you were safe. Despite the fact that from the moment I saw you I felt a connection, a transference of energy that I had never felt with another. Just seeing you, down there, from the water, my body vibrated and I knew there was some tie between us, stronger than the ordinary. But I would never approach you, however, without invitation, without a sign."

"And you received this sign?"

Rodin nodded. They began to walk again.

"When?" asked Monty. "When did you receive a sign?"

"That night on the bridge. When you sang to the water and your tears of sorrow fell into the ripples. I was there, and I sang back to you. Do you not remember? You cried your tears and I tasted them there in the water. There were no words spoken, but the meaning was clear. Your heart was broken, and it broke mine as well. I knew your soul, I had seen it from the very beginning. And, of course, this moment only proved to me that you needed someone to care for it. Someone who would not be careless, but someone who would treasure you."

Monty ran his tongue along his lips. He thought he could taste the saltiness there, as he had that night on the Pont Alexandre.

"You knew all that from just my tears?"

"I could sense more from the start. That night only made me sure. And I wanted to come out of the water then. To hold you, and caress you, and let you know that you would be all right. That love was yours. But I was frightened to show myself because I thought maybe you would be frightened of me. And, somehow I thought, maybe it was too soon then. Too fresh a wound."

Monty smiled. "Yes, had you popped from the river and morphed into a beautiful man, I admit I would have been very disturbed indeed. Even more so than I still was."

Rodin nodded. "The heartbreak lasted some time, and I knew I must wait until your heart was open again. Until I had a chance of overcoming my form and making you realize the love I carried. So I waited. And still I kept watch over you, anticipating when the right moment would come. But, then, one day you were gone. You had left Paris. And it was then that *I* felt heartbroken. I had no way of knowing when or if you would come back. In fact, I did not know if I would ever see you again. And I knew how deeply Trevor had hurt you."

Monty looked at him. "You knew about Trevor specifically?"

"Of course. As I said, you captivated me. I knew you before you knew him; I had been devoted since the first moment I saw. I was there that day at The Sarthe when you swam with your new friend. I nudged you under the water, hoping to get your attention. I dreamed I might distract you, make you see me. But you only had eyes for him that day. So I stayed back, waiting for my time.

Monty leaned against a nearby tree, trying to take it all in. "So you were there even before Trevor?"

"Yes, but I saw your heart was taken by him. And it was not my place to get in the way of that."

Monty sighed. "You know, I wish you had gotten in the way. I think I should have much rather preferred you."

Rodin came to him and put his hands on Monty's waist.

"Do you mean that?" Rodin asked.

"Oh, yes. Very much. You've shown me more kindness and sweetness in one day than all of the men I have known before combined. Even if I fought against it every step of the way. It was all too much to believe, you know. Such passion and graciousness I thought you must have suspicious designs on me."

Rodin smiled. "I did have designs, but they were not suspicious."

He grazed his lips against Monty's and they were kissing. Rodin leaned into the kiss, tenderly, commandingly, devotedly. Rodin place on hand on the trunk of the tree to steady himself, as he used the other to pull Monty's hips against his own. The fires were stoked and the heat began to rise.

Rodin broke away from the kiss leaving Monty gasping and pliant.

"Come to the water with me?" Rodin entreated him.

Monty nodded.

The surface of the Serpentine caught the waning moonlight and it seemed like a giant ball of dim light in the middle of the cove of trees. Just over their tops, Monty could see in the distance the cathedral rising up, silhouetted against the murky sky, its spires like horns adorning a great beast. They stood there together, at the edge of the lake, but watching it silently. Monty felt the cool air drifting from its surface. The cool, wet air, like the mist of a fountain.

"The sea is so vast. All the inlets and rivers and streams and lakes. And yet you found me here," Monty said. "So very far away."

"I was connected to you; I felt you the whole time. Even when you went across the sea, to the new continent, I still had a sense of you. Not as strongly as when you were near, but still enough to feel you were there. As I did my siblings and my mother. Sometimes the feeling wanes, but the bond is never broken. As long as I felt you I knew I could keep searching. It took a long time but finally I found you again."

Monty looked at him. "You have a family then?"

"Yes, but I have not seen them in a long time."

"How long?"

"Too long for me to remember. They were there towards the beginning, but I do not remember it so well. I have been all over, all the time."

"By yourself?"

"Not always. I have not always been alone. I have known others before. And I had brothers and siblings with me once. But then we found our own currents to swim. It is the way."

"How many brothers and sisters do you have?"

"There were seven."

"'Were'?"

Rodin got a faraway look in his eyes and was contemplative, but still he smiled. "Sometimes we end up in the same place or the same time. Not always. The currents get crossed, some are taken far away. But I can always feel them. The ones who have survived, at least."

Monty came close to him then. He touched Rodin's cheek. "You've lost loved ones. I'm very sorry for that."

Rodin grasped his fingers and kissed them. "It was a very long time ago. But now I have you."

"Why in the world did you make such an effort to find me? What do I have to offer?"

Rodin pulled him close. "Everything. You mean everything to me. I see everything about you, and it makes me shine. All those things which you think make you an outsider in this world, those things are beautiful to me. The most beautiful things about you. I have seen the way you care for people, how much you love the ones you cherish. Your tears of sorrow were salty and bitter, but only bitter because they came from such sweetness. I tasted that; I tasted you. I wanted you."

Monty felt his breath catch.

"I listened to your sad song by the river. I know the heart you possess, and it is the only thing that matters to me. I see the person you remain, the heart you continue to carry. Some things are beyond explanation."

Monty felt his emotional resistance give way completely. "Indeed," he said. "If this day has taught me nothing else, it has taught me that much."

"Some things are beyond what we can touch, what we can sense," said Rodin. "What you call magic, why do you not see that it is also love? There is no explanation for love. It is born out of the sea and the air and the stars. It simply is. There is no need to explain what cannot be explained. The way you looked at the sky that night, how they caught by the moonlight as the tears glistened on their surface, I knew you were mine."

They stood, gazing out over the water of the Serpentine together, the light still glistening on its surface.

"Monty?" Rodin said softly.

"Yes?"

"I want to make love to you."

"Now? Here?"

"Yes."

"But we can't, not here."

"Why not?"

"What if someone comes along? What if someone sees us?"

"Then they will see something beautiful."

"They will see something that will get us arrested and thrown into jail, Rodin. This is England, there is a way things work."

Rodin frowned. "England is very frustrating then. Still."

He pulled Monty closer and kissed him. Again, Monty had the sensation that he was suspended in the sea, the rush of the waves crashing through his body. The passion built in their kiss, and Rodin began to unbutton his clothing, slipping his hand under fabric and caressing his skin. The more he touched, his silken touches like vibrations, the more Monty gave in. Around him heard the branches of the trees begin to shake as if blown by a strong wind.

When he opened his eyes again, Rodin was naked and he himself was down to his underclothes. Rodin knelt and peeled the fabric away, his mouth touching all the places the fabric had been, his lips caressing Monty's swollen cock.

"Oh, Rodin," he muttered. "We mustn't."

Rodin broke away and jogged to a nearby tree, stowing their clothes and shoes in the nook of a tree branch.

"Come with me," he said when he returned, extending his hand.

They walked to the edge of the water.

"Kiss me again," says Rodin.

"We certainly can't make love here on the edge of the water," protested Monty.

Rodin laid his finger over Monty's lips. "Do you trust me?"

"Yes, I do. But—"

"Shh. Then kiss me."

Monty kissed him. The kiss again overtook him, and he closed his eyes, reveling in the feeling it gave. He lost himself in the sensation; in his mind, he saw the colors of the sea around him, the shimmering of waves, he felt a tension break deep within and then he was surrounded by warmth and a feeling of ultimate comfort.

When he opened his eyes, he was underwater. With Rodin's arms wrapped around him. He looked around and they were fully submerged. Somehow, as if by magic, he had no trouble breathing, yet and still a crest of panic formed inside him. Rodin laid his finger on his lips and shook his head slowly. He traced the outline of Monty's lips and the motion calmed Monty somewhat. Then Rodin leaned in for another kiss and he felt safe again. He pulled back and motioned for Monty to swim with him. They dove deeper and deeper, foot after foot of water passing them by, their surroundings getting ever darker and darker. Monty clutched Rodin's hand tight and Rodin led the way.

Monty realized, as he swam farther and farther down, that he was no longer afraid. He knew Rodin would protect him. They swam until Rodin stopped and brought them both upright again, floating beside one another. Despite the dark, Monty's eyes had somehow adjusted and he could see Rodin near him. His toes extended beneath him, and Monty shivered as they brushed the sandy bottom. Rodin released him then and the world went to darkness, his sight lost, and for a slight moment, Monty began to panic. But this was cut short as the water around them began to vibrate, flowing and ebbing, as if being pushed away from them in all directions. Monty felt a small drop and realized he was now standing on the floor of the lake, the water around him flowing away. Light broke in somehow, and he could see Rodin before him, spreading out his arms above them both in a semi-circle. The water responded, moving up, and around, until somehow they were standing inside of it. Rodin's motion had fashioned the water into a dome which surrounded them, and a light shone up from the ground, not otherworldly bright, but enough to see in the darkness.

"How is this possible?" whispered Monty, dumbfounded.

Rodin came forward.

"It is possible because it is," said Rodin. "You must believe in magic when you see it before you."

Rodin moved close to Monty and put his arm around Monty's waist, pulling them together. He kissed Monty, deeply and fully. Rodin smelled of seaweed and wind, and tasted of deep, briny salt and Monty treasured every bit. Rodin pulled away from the kiss, and started to move down, but Monty stopped him. Monty wanted to please him, to make him feel as good as Rodin had made him feel with just his words. The entire day, visions of his body had played in Monty's mind and he knew how and where he wanted to start.

He was on his knees then, taking Rodin's magnificent member in his mouth. He ran his tongue slowly up and down its length, and as he heard Rodin moan, he was inspired to move faster and with more determination. Despite its size, Monty took his member to the root and he glanced up to see Rodin throw his arms above his head with an expression of ecstasy. For a brief moment, Monty wondered if his arm motions would bring the water crashing down around them, but he knew he did not care. If the waves fell and drowned him, it would be a moment of exquisiteness that he could not have dreamed up. He devoted all of his attention to Rodin's cock and balls until the man pushed him away, forestalling the end just yet.

Rodin knelt down and began to kiss Monty, moving his mouth over Monty's body until it connected with Monty's cock. He was determined to bring Monty as much pleasure as Monty had brought him and he succeeded. Monty rocked with the motion of Rodin's mouth.

Then Rodin was moving him, laying them both on the sandy, soft lakebed. He grasped Monty's hips and nestled his swollen member against his backside. Monty reached over his shoulder, seeking Rodin's mouth, wanting the feel of his tongue again. They kissed and kissed even as Rodin pressed himself into Monty. Then Rodin was inside him, moving like the sea, deep, penetrating, a rhythm that could not be matched. Monty dug his fingers into the sand, cherishing the rough yet soft feel of it slipping through his fingers. Time took on a new meaning, and he was lost in the sensation for some delicious indeterminable interval. Rodin pulled out of him, turning Monty around, bringing him to rest on his chest.

"Now you for me," whispered Rodin.

He spread his legs then and lifted his haunches from the ground so that Monty could see clearly what he meant. Monty positioned himself and pressed deep inside, rolling his hips, thinking of the crashing of the sea. Face to face, he watched as euphoria spread across Rodin's form, his skin seeming to glow with light, his full, wet lips open in a whimper of supplication. Monty felt them both build to release, and then suddenly, both altogether at once, they were spent. Monty gasped, the vibrations shuddering through him from his scalp to his toes, and he fell against Rodin's glorious chest and buried his face in his neck. A humming escaped his lips, something like a song interspersed with kisses, and he tasted Rodin's skin until he seemed to drift into sleep.

When he opened his eyes next, Monty was lying in the grass on the shore of the Serpentine. He sat up, seeing in the water the smooth, elongated body of a selkie came up, breaking the surface, and then diving back down. Monty laughed, enjoying the playful elation Rodin so obviously felt.

Monty stood, brushing the sand and grass from his skin and ran to his folded clothes. From the inside pocket of his jacket, he removed his small sketchbook. As he returned to the side of the lake, he heard a different sound of splashing. Rodin emerged from the water, fully a man, his neck elongated and his head thrown back gazing at the sky. Naked and stunningly beautiful, his skin had a rosy glow as it reflected the soft rays of the receding night. He swam more around the lake and Monty sketched hurriedly, wanting to record this moment forever.

When Rodin finally emerged from the lake, he approached Monty, extending a hand and pulling him up from the ground.

He gently took the sketchbook from Monty, who did not resist, and studied the page.

"That is me," he said, seemingly in awe.

"Yes, it is, actually."

"It is perfectly captured. As if real life."

"Funny that, isn't it? And thank you."

He pulled Monty to him and kissed him deeply.

"Come now," said Monty. "It will be morning in mere moments."

As they dressed, Monty watched him, the water drying on his skin.

"Rodin." His voice was hesitant. "Being a selkie. Can one become a selkie if one was not born that way?"

Rodin paused and then continued to dress without meeting his eyes.

"It is not something one can just do, it is wide and magical. Maybe even painful."

"There are many things that are painful," Monty said, "which can be endured."

"One should never make decisions like this until one is sure," said Rodin plainly. "It is forever. And forever is forever."

"If it is something magical, then you have demonstrated tonight that you contain much magic."

Rodin's expression was full of affection. "There are many forms of magic, Monty. I do not possess them all."

"That is an assertion I very strongly doubt," said Monty.

He stole a quick kiss as they left the park, the sunrise brilliant and golden and beaming over the lake behind them.

Chapter Fourteen

The morning was crisp and clear; sun fell around them in unfiltered sheets, and there was little by way of clouds or smog jamming the sky, at least by London standards. It was quite simply one of the most marvelous mornings Monty had seen in quite some time. And his mood followed suit—he felt at once satisfied and hopeful.

They would reach the townhouse soon. Monty glanced at Rodin who was smiling and seemed to be enjoying the bright morning as much as he.

"Now that you've had your swim this morning, can you stay like this for long?"

Rodin looked at him affectionately.

"My swim this morning was more for my own amusement. To express the happiness I felt. Yes, the longer I am away from the water, the more I learn to resist the change. Especially if my body and my mind are of one mood. But, of course, I will have to find water on regular occasion."

"We shall have to install a great, large bath then."

"Where shall this be installed?"

"At my apartments," said Monty. "I have a set of rooms just on the other side— Oh, that is, if you would like to visit them some time."

"What about all of the time?"

Monty dipped his head, smiling. "I don't see why that can't be arranged."

They turned the corner and were only a couple of residences away from Bishop's by now.

"But will it prove deleterious in any way? Being so much longer away from the sea than usual?"

Rodin shook his head thoughtfully. "I have known of some who stay away for the remainder of their lives. The only ill effect being that, in that case, life will one day end without visits to the sea. In a standard fashion, that is. They will reach old age."

Monty took that in.

"But will you miss it? The sea?"

"I have been in the sea a very long time. But you I have known little. It is well worth the exchange."

They exchanged a meaningful look.

"Here we are," said Rodin.

"Yes," said Monty, gazing up at the house. "There seem to be some lights on downstairs. Shall we investigate?"

Ever the stalwart, Davies answered the door when they rang.

"Good morning, Davies. Is anyone awake yet?"

"I should not be surprised, Mister Singer, if there are some who have never slept."

They went upstairs, and as they entered their hallway a door opened and out stumbled a half-dressed

Henry, the footman who had been so eager to assist their bathing adventure.

He looked at them, his cheeks flared red, and tried to scuttle by. But he was stopped by a loud, "Wait!" from inside the room.

Anderson Herald, naked, leaned out of the door, grabbing Henry by the front of his trousers, and pulled him in for a kiss.

"Now, bring me some coffee and one of those English breakfasts I hear so much about, won't ya?"

Henry nodded and dashed past Monty and Rodin.

"Fellows," said Anderson. "Good morning."

They nodded their hellos and he retreated, with the unnecessary show of a full turn, back into his room.

They stopped by Bishop's door and found it ajar. Monty pushed it open and discovered Bishop fast asleep on his bed. In a chair nearby, Leggy slept as well. Clearly too knackered to undress properly, he had one shoe on and one off and his head fell against the back of the chair at an awkward angle. He had, however, made sure to tuck Bishop in.

Monty retrieved one of the pillows from Bishop's bed and carefully positioned it behind Leggy's head. The poor man was too exhausted to even stir. Monty covered him with an overcoat that had been tossed on the floor, and then backed out of the room, quietly closing the door behind him.

The next room they came to was Rodin's.

"Here is your room, then," said Monty.

"Yes," Rodin opened the door and paused just inside. "Aren't you coming?"

"Into your room?"

"Yes, of course."

"I am not the type who is usually invited to stay," said Monty.

Rodin pulled him close and kissed his neck.

"Come," Rodin said, "lay by my side."

Inside, they undressed and got into bed. Rodin pulled him close under the covers.

"Rodin?"

"Before you said forever was forever."

"Yes."

"What if I want forever? What if it is all I want?"

Rodin kissed him. "We can talk of forever in the morning."

"But it is morning already."

"Then we can talk of it another time. We have a very long time to plan forever."

Monty traced the curve of his chest. "So you plan to be around for a very long time then?"

"Of course," Rodin answered, his voice teasing. "You do not think I swam all this way only for novelty?"

"I should hope not. I would like to think you came all this way because your heart wouldn't let you go anywhere else."

"Yes. I always follow my heart. And I have followed it to you."

Monty nodded and laid his head on Rodin's chest. Together, they drifted off to sleep, the sound of their breathing murmuring in unison like the soft crash of waves somewhere in the distance.

Author's Note

Thank you for reading! If you have the time to share your thoughts with other readers by leaving a review of this or any other work by Joshua Ian, it would be greatly appreciated. Reviews help boost visibility, which is of utmost importance for independent authors. Feel free to leave your thoughts on Goodreads, Bookbub, or wherever you purchased this eBook.

Copyright

Editing by Deborah Nemeth
Deborah Nemeth Editing Services

Additional Editing by Sue Laybourn
No Stone Unturned Editing Services

http://nostoneunturnedediting.co.uk/

Cover design by Dar Albert
Wicked Smart Designs

https://www.wickedsmartdesigns.com/

Thank you for your support and helping to ensure that all authors can continue to share their work in a fair and rewarding manner.

About the Author

Joshua Ian can easily be captured by a witty turn of phrase or a low-bottomed electronic bassline. If you manage to combine the two, then you have his heart forever. He lives in New York City and is a keen cinema lover and self-proclaimed *Dark Chocolate Expert*. When not staring at a blank screen and cursing the futility of life, he can be found watching cozy mystery shows, daydreaming of his future kaftan collection, or scouring used book vendors to accumulate more vintage romances and mysteries than his shelves are actually capable of handling. One day he plans to travel the world - to see what each country has to offer in the way of used books, movie theatres and dark chocolate, naturally.

Website
moodyboxfan.com

Join the mailing list to keep up-to-date!

Goodreads
https://www.goodreads.com/joshuaian
Facebook
https://www.facebook.com/joshuaianauthor/
Twitter
https://twitter.com/joshuaianauthor
Instagram
https://www.instagram.com/moodyboxfan/
Bookbub
https://www.bookbub.com/authors/joshua-ian
joshuaianauthor@gmail.com

Also by Joshua Ian

DEPARTMENTS OF LOVE SERIES

A brand new historical romance series by Joshua Ian published by Dragonblade Publishing!
Set in Hartridge & Casas, a luxury department store, in Edwardian London.
'The Departments of Love' series features a colorful cast of recurring characters, with each book centering on a different couple, all employees at the store.
Catering to Love (Departments of Love, Book 1)
Fitted to Love (Departments of Love, Book 2)
Stages of Love (Departments of Love, Book 3)

DARKLY ENCHANTED ROMANCE SERIES

(Historical romance with a paranormal edge!)
The Harvest Moon
The Ghost of Hillcomb Hall
Manchester Lake
The Darkly Enchanted Omnibus: A Gothic Romance Collection

Short Stories
All Tall Flowers: A Historical Romance Short
Grave Songs for the Dead: A Short Story Cycle
Gingerbread: A Dark Fiction Short Story
the 1 train: Glimpses of New York City

Keep up-to-date with all of Joshua's current and upcoming projects at moodyboxfan.com

More at Moody Boxfan Books

C heck out these other exciting titles from Moody Boxfan Books!

That Summer in Spain by Lawrence I. Hill

Xavier has booked his break-through film role and he's co-starring with his silver screen crush, Dennis. During the shoot, their feelings blossom into something much deeper than coworkers - but is it just a scorching summer fling or is there more to it? Is Dennis ready to be truthful about himself, and is Xavier really ready to love again?

Déjà Vu: A Holiday Romance Short by Lawrence I. Hill

Another lonely Christmas for hotel director Alvin. When his high school crush - now R&B superstar Tee Mills - comes to stay, things take a turn. Is this a fated chance to rekindle the first love of his life? Alvin isn't sure he's brave enough to find out. But before the night ends, he'll have his answer - if Tee Mills has anything to say about it.